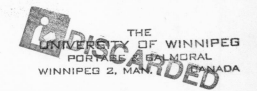

TERMINATIONS

TERMINATIONS

The Death of the Lion
The Coxon Fund
The Middle Years
The Altar of the Dead

BY

HENRY JAMES

Short Story Index Reprint Series

BOOKS FOR LIBRARIES PRESS
FREEPORT, NEW YORK

First Published 1895
Reprinted 1970

INTERNATIONAL STANDARD BOOK NUMBER:
0-8369-3696-5

LIBRARY OF CONGRESS CATALOG CARD NUMBER:
71-134966

PRINTED IN THE UNITED STATES OF AMERICA

CONTENTS

THE DEATH OF THE LION

I

I HAD simply, I suppose, a change of heart, and it must have begun when I received my manuscript back from Mr. Pinhorn. Mr. Pinhorn was my " chief," as he was called in the office ; he had accepted the high mission of bringing the paper up. This was a weekly periodical, and had been supposed to be almost past redemption when he took hold of it. It was Mr. Deedy who had let it down so dreadfully ; he was never mentioned in the office now save in connection with that misdemeanor. Young as I was I had been in a manner taken over from Mr. Deedy, who had been owner as well as editor ; forming part of a promiscuous lot, mainly plant and office furniture, which poor Mrs. Deedy, in her bereavement and depression, parted with at a rough valuation. I could account for my continuity only on the supposition that I had been cheap. I rather resented the practice of fathering all flatness on my late protector, who was in his unhonored grave ; but as I had my way to make, I found matter enough for complacency in being on a " staff." At the same time I was aware

1

that I was exposed to suspicion as a product of the old lowering system. This made me feel that I was doubly bound to have ideas, and had doubtless been at the bottom of my proposing to Mr. Pinhorn that I should lay my lean hands on Neil Paraday. I remember that he looked at me first as if he had never heard of this celebrity, who indeed at that moment was by no means in the centre of the heavens; and even when I had knowingly explained, he expressed but little confidence in the demand for any such matter. When I had reminded him that the great principle on which we were supposed to work was just to create the demand we required, he considered a moment and then rejoined : "I see ; you want to write him up."

"Call it that, if you like."

"And what's your inducement ? "

"Bless my soul—my admiration ! "

Mr. Pinhorn pursed up his mouth. "Is there much to be done with him ? "

"Whatever there is, we should have it all to ourselves, for he hasn't been touched."

This argument was effective, and Mr. Pinhorn responded : "But where can you do it ? "

"Under the fifth rib ! "

Mr. Pinhorn stared. "Where's that ? "

"You want me to go down and see him ? " I enquired, when I had enjoyed his visible search for this obscure suburb.

"I don't ' want ' anything—the proposal's your own. But you must remember that that's the way

we do things *now*," said Mr. Pinhorn, with another
dig at Mr. Deedy.

Unregenerate as I was, I could read the queer
implications of this speech. The present owner's
superior virtue, as well as his deeper craft, spoke
in his reference to the late editor as one of that
baser sort who deal in false representations. Mr.
Deedy would as soon have sent me to call on Neil
Paraday as he would have published a "holiday
number"; but such scruples presented themselves
as mere ignoble thrift to his successor, whose own
sincerity took the form of ringing door-bells, and
whose definition of genius was the art of finding
people at home. It was as if Mr. Deedy had
published reports without his young men's having,
as Pinhorn would have said, really been there. I
was unregenerate, as I have hinted, and I was not
concerned to straighten out the journalistic morals
of my chief, feeling them indeed to be an abyss
over the edge of which it was better not to peer.
Really to be there this time, moreover, was a
vision that made the idea of writing something
subtle about Neil Paraday only the more inspiring.
I would be as considerate as even Mr. Deedy could
have wished, and yet I should be as' present as
only Mr. Pinhorn could conceive. My allusion to
the sequestered manner in which Mr. Paraday
lived (which had formed part of my explanation,
though I knew of it only by hearsay) was, I could
divine, very much what had made Mr. Pinhorn
nibble. It struck him as inconsistent with the

success of his paper that any one should be so
sequestered as that. And, then, was not an immediate exposure of every thing just what the public
wanted? Mr. Pinhorn effectually called me to
order by reminding me of the promptness with
which I had met Miss Braby at Liverpool on her
return from her fiasco in the States. Hadn't we
published, while its freshness and flavor were
unimpaired, Miss Braby's own version of that great
international episode? I felt somewhat uneasy at
this lumping of the actress and the author, and I
confess that, after having enlisted Mr. Pinhorn's
sympathies, I procrastinated a little. I had succeeded better than I wished, and I had, as it happened, work nearer at hand. A few days later I
called on Lord Crouchley, and carried off in triumph the most unintelligible statement that had
yet appeared of his lordship's reasons for his
change of front. I thus set in motion in the daily
papers columns of virtuous verbiage. The following week I ran down to Brighton for a chat, as Mr.
Pinhorn called it, with Mrs. Bounder, who gave
me, on the subject of her divorce, many curious
particulars that had not been articulated in court.
If ever an article flowed from the primal fount it
was that article on Mrs. Bounder. By this time,
however, I became aware that Neil Paraday's new
book was on the point of appearing, and that its
approach had been the ground of my original
appeal to Mr. Pinhorn, who was now annoyed with
me for having lost so many days. He bundled me

off—we would at least not lose another. I have always thought his sudden alertness a remarkable example of the journalistic instinct. Nothing had occurred, since I first spoke to him, to create a visible urgency, and no enlightenment could possibly have reached him. It was a pure case of professional *flair*—he had smelled the coming glory as an animal smells its distant prey.

II

I MAY as well say at once that this little record pretends in no degree to be a picture either of my introduction to Mr. Paraday or of certain proximate steps and stages. The scheme of my narrative allows no space for these things, and in any case a prohibitory sentiment would be attached to my recollection of so rare an hour. These meagre notes are essentially private, so that, if they see the light, the insidious forces that, as my story itself shows, make at present for publicity will simply have overmastered my precautions. The curtain fell lately enough on the lamentable drama. My memory of the day I alighted at Mr. Paraday's door is a fresh memory of kindness, hospitality, compassion, and of the wonderful illuminating talk in which the welcome was conveyed. Some voice of the air had taught me the right moment, the moment of his life in which an act of unexpected young allegiance might most come home. He had recently recovered from a long, grave illness. I had gone to the neighboring inn for the night, but I spent the evening in his company, and he insisted the next day on my sleeping under his roof. I had not an indefinite leave ; Mr. Pinhorn supposed us to put our victims through on the gallop. It was later, in the office, that the dance was set to music. I fortified myself, however, as my training had taught me to do, by the conviction that nothing could be more advantageous for my article than to be written in the very atmosphere. I said nothing to Mr. Paraday about it, but in the morning, after my removal from the inn, while he was occupied in his study, as he had notified me that he should need to be, I committed to paper the quintessence of my impressions. Then thinking to commend myself to Mr. Pinhorn by my celerity, I walked out and posted my little packet before luncheon. Once my paper was written I was free to stay on, and if it was designed to divert attention from my frivolity in so doing, I could reflect with satisfaction that I had never been so clever. I don't mean to deny of course that I was aware it was much too good for Mr. Pinhorn ; but I was equally conscious that Mr. Pinhorn had the supreme shrewdness of recognizing from time to time the cases in which an article was not too bad only because it was too good. There was nothing he loved so much as to print on the right occasion a thing he hated. I had begun my visit to Mr.

Paraday on a Monday, and on the Wednesday his book came out. A copy of it arrived by the first post, and he let me go out into the garden with it immediately after breakfast. I read it from beginning to end that day, and in the evening he asked me to remain with him the rest of the week and over Sunday.

That night my manuscript came back from Mr. Pinhorn, accompanied with a letter, of which the gist was the desire to know what I meant by sending him such stuff. That was the meaning of the question, if not exactly its form, and it made my mistake immense to me. Such as this mistake was, I could now only look it in the face and accept it. I knew where I had failed, but it was exactly where I couldn't have succeeded. I had been sent down there to be personal, and in point of fact I hadn't been personal at all ; what I had sent up to London was just a little finicking, feverish study of my author's talent. Any thing less relevant to Mr. Pinhorn's purpose couldn't well be imagined, and he was visibly angry at my having (at his expense, with a second-class ticket) approached the object of our arrangement only to be so deucedly distant. For myself, I knew but too well what had happened, and how a miracle— as pretty as some old miracle of legend—had been wrought on the spot to save me. There had been a big brush of wings, the flash of an opaline robe, and then, with a great, cool stir of the air, the sense of an angel's having swooped down and

caught me to his bosom. He held me only till
the danger was over, and it all took place in a
minute. With my manuscript back on my hands
I understood the phenomenon better, and the reflections I made on it are what I meant, at the
beginning of this anecdote, by my change of heart.
Mr. Pinhorn's note was not only a rebuke decidedly
stern, but an invitation immediately to send him
(it was the case to say so) the genuine article,
the revealing and reverberating sketch to the
promise of which—and of which alone—I owed
my squandered privilege. A week or two later I
recast my peccant paper, and giving it a particular
application to Mr. Paraday's new book, obtained
for it the hospitality of another journal, where,
I must admit, Mr. Pinhorn was so far justified that
it attracted not the least attention.

III

I WAS frankly, at the end of three days, a very
prejudiced critic, so that one morning when, in the
garden, Neil Paraday had offered to read me something I quite held my breath as I listened. It was
the written scheme of another book—something
he had put aside long ago, before his illness, and
lately taken out again to reconsider. He had been
turning it round when I came down upon him, and
it had grown magnificently under this second hand.

Loose, liberal, confident, it might have passed for a great, gossiping, eloquent letter—the overflow into talk of an artist's amorous plan. The subject I thought singularly rich, quite the strongest he had yet treated ; and this familiar statement of it, full too of fine maturities, was really, in summarized splendor, a mine of gold, a precious, independent work. I remember rather profanely wondering whether the ultimate production could possibly be so happy. His reading of the epistle, at any rate, made me feel as if I were, for the advantage of posterity, in close correspondence with him—were the distinguished person to whom it had been affectionately addressed. It was high distinction simply to be told such things. The idea he now communicated had all the freshness, the flushed fairness of the conception untouched and untried ; it was Venus rising from the sea, before the airs had blown upon her. I had never been so throbbingly present at such an unveiling. But when he had tossed the last bright word after the others, as I had seen cashiers in banks, weighing mounds of coin, drop a final sovereign into the tray, I became conscious of a sudden prudent alarm.

"My dear master, how, after all, are you going to do it ?" I asked. "It's infinitely noble, but what time it will take, what patience and independence, what assured, what perfect conditions it will demand ! Oh, for a lone isle in a tepid sea ! "

"Isn't this practically a lone isle, and aren't you, as an encircling medium, tepid enough ? " he

replied, alluding with a laugh to the wonder of
my young admiration and the narrow limits of his
little provincial home.   "Time isn't what I've
lacked hitherto ; the question hasn't been to find
it, but to use it.   Of course my illness made a
great hole, but I dare say there would have been
a hole at any rate.   The earth we tread has more
pockets than a billiard-table.   The great thing is
now to keep on my feet."

"That's exactly what I mean."

Neil Paraday looked at me with eyes—such
pleasant eyes as he had—in which, as I now recall
their expression, I seem to have seen a dim imagination of his fate.   He was fifty years old, and his
illness had been cruel, his convalescence slow.   "It
isn't as if I weren't all right."

"Oh, if you weren't all right I wouldn't look at
you ! " I tenderly said.

We had both got up, quickened by the full
sound of it all, and he had lighted a cigarette.   I
had taken a fresh one, and, with an intenser smile,
by way of answer to my exclamation, he touched
it with the flame of his match.   "If I weren't
better I shouldn't have thought of *that !* "   He
flourished his epistle in his hand.

"I don't want to be discouraging, but that's not
true," I returned.   "I'm sure that during the
months you lay here in pain you had visitations
sublime.   You thought of a thousand things.   You
think of more and more all the while.   That's
what makes you, if you will pardon my familiarity,

so respectable. At a time when so many people are spent you come into your second wind. But, thank God, all the same, you're better ! Thank God, too, you're not, as you were telling me yesterday, ' successful.' If *you* weren't a failure, what would be the use of trying? That's my one reserve on the subject of your recovery—that it makes you ' score,' as the newspapers say. It looks well in the newspapers, and almost any thing that does that is horrible. ' We are happy to announce that Mr. Paraday, the celebrated author, is again in the enjoyment of excellent health.' Somehow I shouldn't like to see it."

" You won't see it. I'm not in the least celebrated—my obscurity protects me. But couldn't you bear even to see I was dying or dead ? " my companion asked.

" Dead—*passe encore;* there's nothing so safe. One never knows what a living artist may do—one has mourned so many. However, one must make the worst of it ; you must be as dead as you can."

" Don't I meet that condition in having just published a book ? "

" Adequately, let us hope ; for the book is verily a masterpiece."

At this moment the parlor-maid appeared in the door that opened into the garden. Paraday lived at no great cost, and the frisk of petticoats, with a timorous " Sherry, sir ? " was about his modest mahogany. He allowed half his income to his wife, from whom he had succeeded in separating

without redundancy of legend. I had a general
faith in his having behaved well, and I had once,
in London, taken Mrs. Paraday down to dinner.
He now turned to speak to the maid, who offered
him, on a tray, some card or note, while agitated,
excited, I wandered to the end of the garden. The
idea of his security became supremely dear to me,
and I asked myself if I were the same young man
who had come down a few days before to scatter
him to the four winds. When I retraced my steps
he had gone into the house and the woman (the
second London post had come in) had placed my
letters and a newspaper on a bench. I sat down
there to the letters, which were a brief business,
and then, without heeding the address, took the
paper from its envelope. It was the journal of
highest renown, *The Empire* of that morning. It
regularly came to Paraday, but I remembered that
neither of us had yet looked at the copy already
delivered. This one had a great mark on the
" editorial " page, and, uncrumpling the wrapper,
I saw it to be directed to my host and stamped
with the name of his publishers. I instantly
divined that *The Empire* had spoken of him, and
I have not forgotten the odd little shock of the
circumstance. It checked all eagerness and made
me drop the paper, a moment. As I sat there, conscious of a palpitation, I think I had a vision of
what was to be. I had also a vision of the letter
I would presently address to Mr. Pinhorn, breaking,
as it were, with Mr. Pinhorn. Of course, however,

the next minute the voice of *The Empire* was in my ears.

The article was not, I thanked Heaven, a review; it was a "leader," the last of three, presenting Neil Paraday to the human race. His new book, the fifth from his hand, had been but a day or two out, and *The Empire*, already aware of it, fired, as if on the birth of a prince, a salute of a whole column. The guns had been booming these three hours in the house without our suspecting them. The big blundering newspaper had discovered him, and now he was proclaimed and anointed and crowned. His place was assigned him as publicly as if a fat usher with a wand had pointed to the topmost chair; he was to pass up and still up, higher and higher, between the watching faces and the envious sounds—away up to the daïs and the throne. The article was a date; he had taken rank at a bound—waked up a national glory. A national glory was needed, and it was an immense convenience he was there. What all this meant rolled over me, and I fear I grew a little faint—it meant so much more than I could say "yea" to on the spot. In a flash, somehow, all was different; the tremendous wave I speak of had swept something away. It had knocked down, I suppose, my little customary altar, my twinkling tapers and my flowers, and had reared itself into the likeness of a temple vast and bare. When Neil Paraday should come out of the house he would come out a contemporary. That was what had happened; the

poor man was to be squeezed into his horrible age.
I felt as if he had been overtaken on the crest of
the hill and brought back to the city. A little
more, and he would have dipped down the short
cut to posterity and escaped.

IV

WHEN he came out it was exactly as if he had
been in custody, for beside him walked a stout
man with a big black beard, who, save that he
wore spectacles, might have been a policeman, and
in whom at a second glance I recognized the highest contemporary enterprise.

"This is Mr. Morrow," said Paraday, looking, I
thought, rather white ; "he wants to publish
Heaven knows what about me."

I winced as I remembered that this was exactly
what I myself had wanted. "Already ?" I exclaimed, with a sort of sense that my friend had
fled to me for protection.

Mr. Morrow glared, agreeably, through his
glasses ; they suggested the electric headlights
of some monstrous modern ship, and I felt as if
Paraday and I were tossing, terrified, under his
bows. I saw that his momentum was irresistible.
"I was confident that I should be the first in the
field," he declared. "A great interest is naturally
felt in Mr. Paraday's surroundings."

" I hadn't the least idea of it," said Paraday, as
if he had been told he had been snoring.

" I find he has not read the article in *The
Empire*," Mr. Morrow remarked to me. " That's
so very interesting—it's something to start with,"
he smiled. He had begun to pull off his gloves,
which were violently new, and to look encouragingly round the little garden. As a " surrounding "
I felt that I myself had already been taken in ; I
was a little fish in the stomach of a bigger one.
" I represent," our visitor continued, " a syndicate
of influential journals, no less than thirty-seven,
whose public—whose publics, I may say—are in
peculiar sympathy with Mr. Paraday's line of
thought. They would greatly appreciate any expression of his views on the subject of the art he
so brilliantly practises. Besides my connection
with the syndicate just mentioned, I hold a particular commission from *The Tatler*, whose most
prominent department, ' Smatter and Chatter '—I
dare say you've often enjoyed it—attracts such
attention. I was honored only last week, as a
representative of *The Tatler*, with the confidence
of Guy Walsingham, the author of ' Obsessions.'
She expressed herself thoroughly pleased with my
sketch of her method ; she went so far as to say
that I had made her genius more comprehensible
even to herself."

Neil Paraday had dropped upon the garden-
'bench, and sat there at once detached and confused ; he looked hard at a bare spot in the lawn,

as if with an anxiety that had suddenly made him grave. His movement had been interpreted by his visitor as an invitation to sink sympathetically into a wicker chair that stood hard by, and as Mr. Morrow so settled himself I felt that he had taken official possession and that there was no undoing it. One had heard of unfortunate people's having "a man in the house," and this was just what we had. There was a silence of a moment, during which we seemed to acknowledge in the only way that was possible the presence of universal fate ; the sunny stillness took no pity, and my thought, as I was sure Paraday's was doing, performed within the minute a great distant revolution. I saw just how emphatic I should make my rejoinder to Mr. Pinhorn, and that, having come, like Mr. Morrow, to betray, I must remain as long as possible to save. Not because I had brought my mind back, but because our visitor's last words were in my ear, I presently enquired, with gloomy irrelevance, if Guy Walsingham were a woman.

" Oh, yes ! a mere pseudonym; but convenient, you know, for a lady who goes in for the larger latitude. ' Obsessions, by Miss So-and-so,' would look a little odd, but men are more naturally indelicate. Have you peeped into ' Obsessions ' ? " Mr. Morrow continued sociably to our companion.

Paraday, still absent, remote, made no answer, as if he had not heard the question: a manifestation that appeared to suit the cheerful Mr. Morrow as well as any other. Imperturbably bland, he was

a man of resources—he only needed to be on
the spot. He had pocketed the whole poor place
while Paraday and I were wool-gathering, and I
could imagine that he had already got his "heads."
His system, at any rate, was justified by the inevi-
tability with which I replied, to save my friend
the trouble : "Dear, no ! he hasn't read it. He
doesn't read such things ! " I unwarily added.

"Things that are *too* far over the fence, eh ? "
I was indeed a godsend to Mr. Morrow. It was
the psychological moment ; it determined the appearance of his notebook, which, however, he at
first kept slightly behind him, even as the dentist,
approaching his victim, keeps the horrible forceps.
"Mr. Paraday holds with the good old proprieties
—I see ! " And thinking of the thirty-seven influential journals, I found myself, as I found poor
Paraday, helplessly gazing at the promulgation
of this ineptitude. "There's no point on which
distinguished views are so acceptable as on this
question—raised perhaps more strikingly than
ever by Guy Walsingham—of the permissibility
of the larger latitude. I have an appointment precisely in connection with it, next week, with Dora
Forbes, the author of 'The Other Way Round,'
which every-body is talking about. Has Mr.
Paraday glanced at 'The Other Way Round '? "
Mr. Morrow now frankly appealed to me. I took
upon myself to repudiate the supposition, while
our companion, still silent, got up nervously and
walked away. His visitor paid no heed to his

2

withdrawal ; he only opened out the notebook with a more motherly pat. "Dora Forbes, I gather, takes the ground, the same as Guy Walsingham's, that the larger latitude has simply got to come. He holds that it has got to be squarely faced. Of course his sex makes him a less prejudiced witness. But an authoritative word from Mr. Paraday—from the point of view of *his* sex, you know, would go right round the globe. He takes the line that we *haven't* got to face it ? "

I was bewildered : it sounded somehow as if there were three sexes. My interlocutor's pencil was poised, my private responsibility great. I simply sat staring, however, and only found presence of mind to say : " Is this Miss Forbes a gentleman ? "

Mr. Morrow hesitated an instant, smiling.   " It wouldn't be ' Miss '—there's a wife ! "

" I mean is she a man ? "

" The wife ? "—Mr. Morrow, for a moment, was as confused as myself.   But, when I explained that I alluded to Dora Forbes in person, he informed me, with visible amusement at my being so out of it, that this was the " pen-name " of an indubitable male—he had a big red mustache.   " He only assumes a feminine personality because the ladies are such popular favorites.   A great deal of interest is felt in this assumption, and there's every prospect of its being widely imitated."   Our host at this moment joined us again, and Mr. Morrow remarked invitingly that he should be happy to make a note of any observation the movement in question, the bid for success under a lady's name, might suggest to Mr. Paraday. But the poor man, without catching the allusion, excused himself, pleading that, though he was greatly honored by the visitor's interest, he suddenly felt unwell and should have to take leave of him—have to go and lie down and keep quiet. His young friend might be trusted to answer for him, but he hoped Mr. Morrow didn't expect great things even of his young friend. His young friend, at this moment, looked at Neil Paraday with an anxious eye, greatly wondering if he were doomed to be ill again ; but Paraday's own kind face met his question reassuringly, seemed to say in a glance intelligible enough : "Oh, I'm not ill, but I'm scared : get him out of the house as quietly as possible." Getting newspaper-men out of the house was odd business for an emissary of Mr. Pinhorn, and I was so exhilarated by the idea of it that I called after him as he left us :

"Read the article in *The Empire*, and you'll soon be all right ! "

V

"DELICIOUS, my having come down to tell him of it ! " Mr. Morrow ejaculated. " My cab was at the door twenty minutes after *The Empire* had been laid upon my breakfast table. Now, what have you got for me?" he continued, dropping again into his chair, from which, however, the next moment he quickly rose. "I was shown into the drawing-room, but there must be more to see—his study, his literary sanctum, the little things he has about, or other domestic objects or features. He wouldn't be lying down on his study-table? There's a great interest always felt in the scene of an author's labors. Sometimes we're favored with very delightful peeps. Dora Forbes showed me all his table-drawers, and almost jammed my hand into one into which I made a dash! I don't ask that of you, but if we could talk things over right there where he sits I feel as if I should get the key-note."

I had no wish whatever to be rude to Mr. Morrow, I was much too initiated not to prefer the safety of other ways; but I had a quick inspiration, and I entertained an insurmountable, an almost superstitious objection to his crossing the threshold of my friend's little lonely, shabby, consecrated workshop. "No, no—we sha'n't get at his life that way," I said. "The way to get at his life is to —but wait a moment!" I broke off and went quickly into the house; then, in three minutes, I reappeared before Mr. Morrow with the two volumes of Paraday's new book. "His life's here," I went on, "and I'm so full of this admirable thing that I can't talk of any thing else. The artist's life's his work, and this is the place to observe him. What he has to tell us he tells with *this* perfection. My dear sir, the best interviewer's the best reader.".

Mr. Morrow good-humoredly protested. "Do you mean to say that no other source of information should be open to us?"

"None other till this particular one—by far the most copious—has been quite exhausted. Have you exhausted it, my dear sir? Had you exhausted it when you came down here? It seems to me in our time almost wholly neglected, and something should surely be done to restore its ruined credit. It's the course to which the artist himself at every step, and with such pathetic confidence, refers us. This last book of Mr. Paraday's is full of revelations."

"Revelations?" panted Mr. Morrow, whom I had forced again into his chair.

"The only kind that count. It tells you with a perfection that seems to me quite final all the author thinks, for instance, about the advent of the ' larger latitude.' "

"Where does it do that?" asked Mr. Morrow, who had picked up the second volume and was insincerely thumbing it.

"Everywhere—in the whole treatment of his case. Extract the opinion, disengage the answer —those are the real acts of homage."

Mr. Morrow, after a minute, tossed the book away. "Ah! but you mustn't take me for a reviewer."

"Heaven forbid I should take you for any thing

so dreadful ! You came down to perform a little
act of sympathy, and so, I may confide to you,
did I.   Let us perform our little act together.
These pages overflow with the testimony we want:
let us read them and taste them and interpret them.
You will of course have perceived for yourself that
one scarcely does read Neil Paraday till one reads
him aloud; he gives out to the ear an extraordinary
quality, and it's only when you expose it confidently
to that test that you really get near his style. Take
up your book again and let me listen, while you
pay it out, to that wonderful fifteenth chapter. If
you feel that you can't do it justice, compose
yourself to attention while I produce for you—I
think I can—this scarcely less admirable ninth."

Mr. Morrow gave me a straight glance which
was as hard as a blow between the eyes ; he had
turned rather red, and a question had formed itself
in his mind which reached my sense as distinctly
as if he had uttered it : " What sort of a d——d
fool are *you?* " Then he got up, gathering together his hat and gloves, buttoning his coat,
projecting hungrily all over the place the big trans-
parency of his mask. It seemed to flare over Fleet
Street and somehow made the actual spot distress-
ingly humble : there was so little for it to feed on
unless he counted the blisters of our stucco or saw
his way to do something with the roses. Even the
poor roses were common kinds. Presently his
eyes fell upon the manuscript from which Paraday
had been reading to me and which still lay on the

bench. As my own followed them I saw that it looked promising, looked pregnant, as if it gently throbbed with the life the reader had given it. Mr. Morrow indulged in a nod toward it and a vague thrust of his umbrella. " What's that ? "

" Oh, it's a plan—a secret."

" A secret ! " There was an instant's silence, and then Mr. Morrow made another movement. I may have been mistaken, but it affected me as the translated impulse of the desire to lay hands on the manuscript, and this led me to indulge in a quick, anticipatory grab which may very well have seemed ungraceful, or even impertinent, and which at any rate left Mr. Paraday's two admirers very erect, glaring at each other, while one of them held a bundle of papers well behind him. An instant later Mr. Morrow quitted me abruptly, as if he had really carried something off with him. To reassure myself, watching his broad back recede, I only grasped my manuscript the tighter. He went to the back-door of the house, the one he had come out from, but on trying the handle he appeared to find it fastened. So he passed round into the front garden, and by listening intently enough I could presently hear the outer gate close behind him with a bang. I thought again of the thirty-seven influential journals and wondered what would be his revenge. I hasten to add that he was magnanimous ; which was just the most dreadful thing he could have been. *The Tatler* published a charming, chatty, familiar account of Mr. Paraday's

" Home-life," and on the wings of the thirty-seven
influential journals it went, to use Mr. Morrow's
own expression, right round the globe.

VI

A week later, early in May, my glorified friend
came up to town, where, it may be veraciously
recorded, he was the king of the beasts of the year.
No advancement was ever more rapid, no exaltation more complete, no bewilderment more teach-
able. His book sold but moderately, though the
article in *The Empire* had done unwonted wonders
for it ; but he circulated in person in a manner
that the libraries might well have envied. His
formula had been found—he was a " revelation."
His momentary terror had been real, just as mine
had been—the overclouding of his passionate desire
to be left to finish his work. He was far from
unsociable, but he had the finest conception of
being let alone that I have ever met. For the
time, however, he took his profit where it seemed
most to crowd upon him, having in his pocket the
portable sophistries about the nature of the artist's
task. Observation too was a kind of work and
experience a kind of success ; London dinners were
all material and London ladies were fruitful toil.
" No one has the faintest conception of what I'm
trying for," he said to me, " and not many have

read three pages that I've written ; but I must dine with them first—they'll find out why when they've time." It was rather rude justice, perhaps ; but the fatigue had the merit of being a new sort, and the phantasmagoric town was probably after all less of a battlefield than the haunted study. He once told me that he had had no personal life to speak of since his fortieth year, but had had more than was good for him before. London closed the parenthesis and exhibited him in relations ; one of the most inevitable of these being that in which he found himself to Mrs. Weeks Wimbush, wife of the boundless brewer and proprietress of the universal menagerie. In this establishment, as every-body knows, on occasions when the crush is great, the animals rub shoulders freely with the spectators and the lions sit down for whole evenings with the lambs.

It had been ominously clear to me from the first that in Neil Paraday this lady, who, as all the world agreed, was tremendous fun, considered that she had secured a prime attraction, a creature of almost heraldic oddity. Nothing could exceed her enthusiasm over her capture, and nothing could exceed the confused apprehensions it excited in me. I had an instinctive fear of her which I tried without effect to conceal from her victim, but which I let her perceive with perfect impunity. Paraday heeded it, but she never did, for her conscience was that of a romping child. She was a blind, violent force, to which I could attach no more idea of responsibility than to the creaking of a sign in the wind. It was difficult to say what she conduced to but to circulation. She was constructed of steel and leather, and all I asked of her for our tractable friend was not to do him to death. He had consented for a time to be of india-rubber, but my thoughts were fixed on the day he should resume his shape or at least get back into his box. It was evidently all right, but I should be glad when it was well over. I had a special fear—the impression was ineffaceable of the hour when, after Mr. Morrow's departure, I had found him on the sofa in his study. That pretext of indisposition had not in the least been meant as a snub to the envoy of *The Tatler*—he had gone to lie down in very truth. He had felt a pang of his old pain, the result of the agitation wrought in him by this forcing open of a new period. His old programme, his old ideal even had to be changed. Say what one would, success was a complication and recognition had to be reciprocal. The monastic life, the pious illumination of the missal in the convent cell were things of the gathered past. It didn't engender despair, but it at least required adjustment. Before I left him on that occasion we had passed a bargain, my part of which was that I should make it my business to take care of him. Let whoever would represent the interest in his presence (I had a mystical prevision of Mrs. Weeks Wimbush) I should represent the interest in his work—in other words in his absence. These

two interests were in their essence opposed ; and
I doubt, as youth is fleeting, if I shall ever again
know the intensity of joy with which I felt that in
so good a cause I was willing to make myself
odious.

One day, in Sloane Street, I found myself ques-
tioning Paraday's landlord, who had come to the
door in answer to my knock. Two vehicles, a
barouche and a smart hansom, were drawn up before the house.

"In the drawing-room, sir ? Mrs. Weeks Wimbush."

"And in the dining-room ? "

"A young lady, sir—waiting : I think a for-
eigner."

It was three o'clock, and on days when Paraday
didn't lunch out he attached a value to these sub-
jugated hours. On which days, however, didn't
the dear man lunch out ? Mrs. Wimbush, at such
a crisis, would have rushed round immediately
after her own repast. I went into the dining-room
first, postponing the pleasure of seeing how, up-
stairs, the lady of the barouche would, on my
arrival, point the moral of my sweet solicitude.
No one took such an interest as herself in his
doing only what was good for him, and she was
always on the spot to see that he did it. She
made appointments with him to discuss the best
means of economizing his time and protecting his
privacy. She further made his health her special
business, and had so much sympathy with my own

zeal for it that she was the author of pleasing fictions on the subject of what my devotion had led me to give up. I gave up nothing (I don't count Mr. Pinhorn) because I had nothing, and all I had as yet achieved was to find myself also in the menagerie. I had dashed in to save my friend, but I had only got domesticated and wedged ; so that I could do nothing for him but exchange with him over people's heads looks of intense but futile intelligence.

VII

THE young lady in the dining-room had a brave face, black hair, blue eyes, and in her lap a big volume. " I've come for his autograph," she said, when I had explained to her that I was under bonds to see people for him when he was occupied. " I've been waiting half an hour, but I'm prepared to wait all day." I don't know whether it was this that told me she was American, for the propensity to wait all day is not in general characteristic of her race. I was enlightened probably not so much by the spirit of the utterance as by some quality of its sound. At any rate I saw she had an individual patience and a lovely frock, together with an expression that played among her pretty features like a breeze among flowers. Putting her book upon the table, she showed me a massive album, showily bound and full of autographs of price. The collection of faded notes, of still more faded "thoughts," of quotations, platitudes, signatures, represented a formidable purpose.

"Most people apply to Mr. Paraday by letter, you know," I said.

"Yes, but he doesn't answer. I've written three times."

"Very true," I reflected; "the sort of letter you mean goes straight into the fire."

"How do you know the sort I mean?" My interlocutress had blushed and smiled, and in a moment she added: "I don't believe he gets many like them!"

"I'm sure they're beautiful, but he burns without reading." I didn't add that I had told him he ought to.

"Isn't he then in danger of burning things of importance?"

"He would be, if distinguished men hadn't an infallible nose for nonsense."

She looked at me a moment—her face was sweet and gay. "Do *you* burn without reading, too?" she asked; in answer to which I assured her that, if she would trust me with her repository, I would see that Mr. Paraday should write his name in it.

She considered a little. "That's very well, but it wouldn't make me see him."

"Do you want very much to see him?" It seemed ungracious to catechise so charming a creature, but somehow I had never yet taken my duty to the great author so seriously.

"Enough to have come from America for the purpose."

I stared. "All alone?"

"I don't see that that's exactly your business; but if it will make me more appealing I'll confess that I'm quite by myself. I had to come alone or not come at all."

She was interesting; I could imagine that she had lost parents, natural protectors—could conceive even that she had inherited money. I was in a phase of my own fortune when keeping hansoms at doors seemed to me pure swagger. As a trick of this bold and sensitive girl, however, it became romantic—a part of the general romance of her freedom, her errand, her innocence. The confidence of young Americans was notorious, and I speedily arrived at a conviction that no impulse could have been more generous than the impulse that had operated here. I foresaw at that moment that it would make her my peculiar charge, just as circumstances had made Neil Paraday. She would be another person to look after, and one's honor would be concerned in guiding her straight. These things became clearer to me later; at the instant I had scepticism enough to observe to her, as I turned the pages of her volume, that her net had, all the same, caught many a big fish. She appeared to have had fruitful access to the great ones of the earth; there were people, moreover, whose signatures she had presumably secured without a personal interview. She couldn't have worried George Washington and Friedrich Schiller and Hannah More.   She met this argument, to my surprise, by throwing up the album without a pang.   It wasn't even her own ; she was responsible for none of its treasures.   It belonged to a girl-friend in America, a young lady in a Western city. This young lady had insisted on her bringing it, to pick up more autographs ; she thought they might like to see, in Europe, in what company they would be.   The " girl-friend," the Western city, the immortal names, the curious errand, the idyllic faith, all made a story as strange to me, and as beguiling, as some tale in the Arabian Nights. Thus it was that my informant had encumbered herself with the ponderous tome ; but she hastened to assure me that this was the first time she had brought it out.   For her visit to Mr. Paraday it had simply been a pretext.   She didn't really care a straw that he should write his name ; what she did want was to look straight into his face.

I demurred a little.   " And why do you require to do that ? "

" Because I just love him ! "   Before I could recover from the agitating effect of this crystal ring my companion had continued : " Hasn't there ever been any face that you've wanted to look into ? "

How could I tell her so soon how much I appreciated the opportunity of looking into hers ?   I could only assent in general to the proposition that there were certainly for every one such hanker-

ings, and even such faces ; and I felt that the
crisis demanded all my lucidity, all my wisdom.
"Oh, yes ! I'm a student of physiognomy. Do you
mean," I pursued, "that you've a passion for Mr.
Paraday's books ? "

"They've been every thing to me, and a little
more beside—I know them by heart. They've
completely taken hold of me. There's no author
about whom I feel as I do about Neil Paraday."

"Permit me to remark then," I presently rejoined, "that you're one of the right sort."

"One of the enthusiasts ? Of course I am ! "

"Oh, there are enthusiasts who are quite of the
wrong. I mean you're one of those to whom an
appeal can be made."

"An appeal ? " Her face lighted as if with the
chance of some great sacrifice.

If she was ready for one it was only waiting for
her, and in a moment I mentioned it. "Give up
this crude purpose of seeing him. Go away without it. That will be far better."

She looked mystified ; then she turned visibly
pale. "Why, hasn't he any personal charm ? "
The girl was terrible and laughable in her bright
directness.

"Ah, that dreadful word 'personal' ! " I exclaimed ; "we're dying of it, and you women bring
it out with murderous effect. When you en-
counter a genius as fine as this idol of ours, let
him off the dreary duty of being a personality as

well. Know him only by what's best in him, and
spare him for the same sweet sake."

My young lady continued to look at me in confusion and mistrust, and the result of her reflection
on what I had just said was to make her suddenly
break out : "Look here, sir—what's the matter
with him ? "

"The matter with him is that, if he doesn't look
out, people will eat a great hole in his life."

She considered a moment. " He hasn't any disfigurement ? "

"Nothing to speak of ! "

"Do you mean that social engagements inter-
fere with his occupations ? "

"That but feebly expresses it."

"So that he can't give himself up to his beautiful
imagination ? "

" He's badgered, bothered, overwhelmed, on the
pretext of being applauded. People expect him to
give them his time, his golden time, who would
not themselves give five shillings for one of his
books."

" Five ? I'd give five thousand ! "

" Give your sympathy—give your forbearance.
Two-thirds of those who approach him only do it
to advertise themselves."

"Why, it's too bad ! " the girl exclaimed, with
the face of an angel. " It's the first time I was
ever called crude ! " she laughed.

I followed up my advantage. " There's a lady
with him now who's a terrible complication, and

3

who yet hasn't read, I am sure, ten pages that he ever wrote."

My visitor's wide eyes grew tenderer. "Then how does she talk——"

"Without ceasing. I only mention her as a single case. Do you want to know how to show a superlative consideration? Simply avoid him."

"Avoid him?" she softly wailed.

"Don't force him to have to take account of you; admire him in silence, cultivate him at a distance and secretly appropriate his message. Do you want to know," I continued, warming to my idea, "how to perform an act of homage really sublime?" Then, as she hung on my words: "Succeed in never seeing him at all!"

"Never at all?" she pathetically gasped.

"The more you get into his writings the less you'll want to; and you'll be immensely sustained by the thought of the good you're doing him."

She looked at me without resentment or spite, and at the truth I had put before her with candor, credulity, pity. I was afterward happy to remember that she must have recognized in my face the liveliness of my interest in herself. "I think I see what you mean."

"Oh, I express it badly; but I should be delighted if you would let me come to see you—to explain it better."

She made no response to this, and her thoughtful eyes fell on the big album, on which she presently laid her hands as if to take it away. "I did use to

say out West that they might write a little less for
autographs (to all the great poets, you know) and
study the thoughts and style a little more."

"What do they care for the thoughts and style?
They didn't even understand you. I'm not sure,"
I added, "that I do myself, and I dare say that you
by no means make me out." She had got up to
go, and though I wanted her to succeed in not seeing Neil Paraday I wanted her also, inconsequently,
to remain in the house. I was at any rate far
from desiring to hustle her off. As Mrs. Weeks
Wimbush, upstairs, was still saving our friend in
her own way, I asked my young lady to let me
briefly relate, in illustration of my point, the little
incident of my having gone down into the country
for a profane purpose and been converted on the
spot to holiness. Sinking again into her chair to
listen, she showed a deep interest in the anecdote.
Then, thinking it over gravely, she exclaimed,
with her odd intonation :

"Yes, but you do see him !" I had to admit
that this was the case ; and I was not so prepared
with an effective attenuation as I could have
wished. She eased the situation off, however, by
the charming quaintness with which she finally
said : "Well, I wouldn't want him to be lonely !"
This time she rose in earnest, but I persuaded her
to let me keep the album to show to Mr. Paraday.
I assured her I would bring it back to her myself.
"Well, you'll find my address somewhere in it, on
a paper !" she sighed resignedly, at the door.

VIII

I BLUSH to confess it, but I invited Mr. Paraday that very day to transcribe into the album one of his most characteristic passages. I told him how I had got rid of the strange girl who had brought it—her ominous name was Miss Hurter, and she lived at an hotel; quite agreeing with him, moreover, as to the wisdom of getting rid with equal promptitude of the book itself. This was why I carried it to Albemarle Street no later than on the morrow. I failed to find her at home, but she wrote to me and I went again: she wanted so much to hear more about Neil Paraday. I returned repeatedly, I may briefly declare, to supply her with this information. She had been immensely taken, the more she thought of it, with that idea of mine about the act of homage: it had ended by filling her with a generous rapture. She positively desired to do something sublime for him, though indeed I could see that, as this particular flight was difficult, she appreciated the fact that my visits kept her up. I had it on my conscience to keep her up; I neglected nothing that would contribute to it, and her conception of our cherished author's independence became at last as fine as his own conception. " Read him, read

him," I constantly repeated ; while, seeking him
in his works, she represented herself as convinced
that, according to my assurance, this was the
system that had, as she expressed it, weaned her.
We read him together when I could find time, and
the generous creature's sacrifice was fed by our
conversation. There were twenty selfish women,
about whom I told her, who stirred her with a
beautiful rage. Immediately after my first visit
her sister, Mrs. Milsom, came over from Paris, and
the two ladies began to present, as they called it,
their letters. I thanked our stars that none had
been presented to Mr. Paraday. They received
invitations and dined out, and some of these occasions enabled Fanny Hurter to perform, for con-
sistency's sake, touching feats of submission.
Nothing indeed would now have induced her even
to look at the object of her admiration. Once,
hearing his name announced at a party, she
instantly left the room by another door and then
straightway quitted the house. At another time,
when I was at the opera with them (Mrs. Milsom
had invited me to their box), I attempted to point
Mr. Paraday out to her in the stalls. On this she
asked her sister to change places with her, and
while that lady devoured the great man through a
powerful glass, presented, all the rest of the evening, her inspired back to the house. To torment
her tenderly I pressed the glass upon her, telling
her how wonderfully near it brought our friend's
handsome head. By way of answer she simply

looked at me in charged silence, letting me see that tears had gathered in her eyes. These tears, I may remark, produced an effect on me of which the end is not yet. There was a moment when I felt it my duty to mention them to Neil Paraday; but I was deterred by the reflection that there were questions more relevant to his happiness.

These questions, indeed, by the end of the season were reduced to a single one—the question of re-constituting, so far as might be possible, the conditions under which he had produced his best work. Such conditions could never all come back, for there was a new one that took up too much place ; but some perhaps were not beyond recall. I wanted above all things to see him sit down to the subject of which, on my making his acquaintance, he had read me that admirable sketch. Something told me there was no security but in his doing so before the new factor, as we used to say at Mr. Pinhorn's, should render the problem incalculable. It only half reassured me that the sketch itself was so copious and so eloquent that even at the worst there would be the making of a small but complete book, a tiny volume which, for the faithful, might well become an object of adoration. There would even not be wanting critics to declare, I foresaw, that the plan was a thing to be more thankful for than the structure to have been reared on it. My impatience for the structure, none the less, grew and grew with the interruptions. He had, on coming up to town, begun to sit for his portrait to a young painter, Mr.

Rumble, whose little game, as we also used to say at Mr. Pinhorn's, was to be the first to perch on the shoulders of renown. Mr. Rumble's studio was a circus in which the man of the hour, and still more the woman, leaped through the hoops of his showy frames almost as electrically as they burst into telegrams and " specials." He pranced into the exhibitions on their back ; he was the reporter on canvas, the Vandyke up to date, and there was one roaring year in which Mrs. Bounder and Mrs. Braby, Guy Walsingham and Dora Forbes, proclaimed in chorus from the same pictured walls that no one had yet got ahead of him.

Paraday had been promptly caught and saddled, accepting with characteristic good-humor his confidential hint that to figure in his show was not so much a consequence as a cause of immortality. From Mrs. Wimbush to the last "representative" who called to ascertain his twelve favorite dishes, it was the same ingenuous assumption that he would rejoice in the repercussion. There were moments when I fancied I might have had more patience with them if they had not been so fatally benevolent. I hated, at all events, Mr. Rumble's picture, and had my bottled resentment ready when, later on, I found my distracted friend had been stuffed by Mrs. Wimbush into the mouth of another cannon. A young artist in whom she was intensely interested, and who had no connection with Mr. Rumble, was to show how far he could make him go. Poor Paraday, in return, was naturally to write something somewhere about the young artist. She played her victims against each other with admirable ingenuity, and her establishment was a huge machine in which the tiniest and the biggest wheels went round to the same treadle. I had a scene with her in which I tried to express that the function of such a man was to exercise his genius—not to serve as a hoarding for pictorial posters. The people I was perhaps angriest with were the editors of magazines who had introduced what they called new features, so aware were they that the newest feature of all would be to make him grind their axes by contributing his views on vital topics and taking part in the periodical prattle about the future of fiction. I made sure that before I should have done with him there would scarcely be a current form of words left me to be sick of ; but meanwhile I could make surer still of my animosity to bustling ladies for whom he drew the water that irrigated their social flower-beds.

I had a battle with Mrs. Wimbush over the artist she protected, and another over the question of a certain week, at the end of July, that Mr. Paraday appeared to have contracted to spend with her in the country. I protested against this visit ; I intimated that he was too unwell for hospitality without a *nuance,* for caresses without imagination ; I begged he might rather take the time in some restorative way. A sultry air of promises, of ponderous parties, hung over his August, and he would greatly profit by the interval of rest. He had not told me he was

ill again—that he had had a warning ; but I had
not needed this, and I found his reticence his worst
symptom. The only thing he said to me was that
he believed a comfortable attack of something or
other would set him up ; it would put out of the
question every thing but the exemptions he prized.
I am afraid I shall have presented him as a martyr
in a very small cause if I fail to explain that he
surrendered himself much more liberally than I surrendered him. He filled his lungs, for the most
part, with the comedy of his queer fate ; the tragedy
was in the spectacles through which I chose to look.
He was conscious of inconvenience, and above all
of a great renouncement ; but how could he have
heard a mere dirge in the bells of his accession ?
The sagacity and the jealousy were mine, and his
the impressions and the anecdotes. Of course, as
regards Mrs. Wimbush, I was worsted in my en-
counters, for was not the state of his health the
very reason for his coming to her at Prestidge ?
Wasn't it precisely at Prestidge that he was to be
coddled, and wasn't the dear princess coming to
help her to coddle him ? The dear princess, now on
a visit to England, was of a famous foreign house,
and, in her gilded cage, with her retinue of keepers
and feeders, was the most expensive specimen in
the good lady's collection. I don't think her august
presence had had to do with Paraday's consenting
to go, but it is not impossible that he had operated
as a bait to the illustrious stranger. The party had
been made up for him, Mrs. Wimbush averred, and

every one was counting on it, the dear princess most of all. If he was well enough he was to read them something absolutely fresh, and it was on that particular prospect the princess had set her heart. She was so fond of genius in *any* walk of life, and she was so used to it, and understood it so well ; she was the greatest of Mr. Paraday's admirers, she devoured every thing he wrote. And then he read like an angel. Mrs. Wimbush reminded me that he had again and again given her, Mrs. Wimbush, the privilege of listening to him.

I looked at her a moment. " What has he read to you ? " I crudely enquired.

For a moment too she met my eyes, and for the fraction of a moment she hesitated and colored. " Oh, all sorts of things ! "

I wondered whether this were an imperfect recollection or only a perfect fib, and she quite understood my unuttered comment on her perception of such things. But if she could forget Neil Paraday's beauties she could of course forget my rudeness, and three days later she invited me, by telegraph, to join the party at Prestidge. This time she might indeed have had a story about what I had given up to be near the master. I addressed from that fine residence several communications to a young lady in London, a young lady whom, I confess, I quitted with reluctance, and whom the reminder of what she herself could give up was required to make me quit at all. It adds to the gratitude I owe her on other grounds that she kindly allows me to transcribe from my letters a few of the passages in which that hateful sojourn is candidly commemorated.

IX

"I SUPPOSE I ought to enjoy the joke of what's going on here," I wrote, "but somehow it doesn't amuse me. Pessimism on the contrary possesses me and cynicism solicits. I positively feel my own flesh sore from the brass nails in Neil Paraday's social harness. The house is full of people who like him, as they mention, awfully, and with whom his talent for talking nonsense has prodigious success. I delight in his nonsense myself; why is it therefore that I grudge these happy folk their artless satisfaction? Mystery of the human heart—abyss of the critical spirit! Mrs. Wimbush thinks she can answer that question, and, as my want of gayety has at last worn out her patience, she has given me a glimpse of her shrewd guess. I am made restless by the selfishness of the insincere friend—I want to monopolize Paraday in order that he may push me on. To be intimate with him is a feather in my cap; it gives me an importance that I couldn't naturally pretend to, and I seek to deprive him of social refreshment because I fear that meeting more disinterested people may enlighten him as to my real motive. All the dis-

interested people here are his particular admirers
and have been carefully selected as such. There
is supposed to be a copy of his last book in the
house, and in the hall I come upon ladies, in
attitudes, bending gracefully over the first volume.
I discreetly avert my eyes, and when I next look
round the precarious joy has been superseded by
the book of life. There is a sociable circle or a
confidential couple, and the relinquished volume
lies open on its face, as if it had been dropped
under extreme coercion. Somebody else presently
finds it and transfers it, with its air of momentary
desolation, to another piece of furniture. Every
one is asking every one about it all day, and every
one is telling every one where they put it last.
I'm sure it's rather smudgy about the twentieth
page. I have a strong impression too that the
second volume is lost—has been packed in the bag
of some departing guest ; and yet every-body has
the impression that somebody else has read to the
end. You see therefore that the beautiful book
plays a great part in our conversation. Why
should I take the occasion of such distinguished
honors to say that I begin to see deeper into
Gustave Flaubert's doleful refrain about the hatred
of literature ? I refer you again to the perverse
constitution of man.

" The princess is a massive lady with the organi-
zation of an athlete and the confusion of tongues
of a *valet de place*. She contrives to commit herself extraordinarily little in a great many languages,

and is entertained and conversed with in detach-
ments and relays, like an institution which goes on
from generation to generation or a big building
contracted for under a forfeit. She can't have a
personal taste any more than, when her husband
succeeds, she can have a personal crown, and her
opinion on any matter is rusty and heavy and
plain—made, in the night of ages, to last and be
transmitted. I feel as if I ought to pay some one
a fee for my glimpse of it. She has been told
every thing in the world and has never perceived
anything, and the echoes of her education respond
awfully to the rash footfall—I mean the casual
remark—in the cold Valhalla of her memory.
Mrs. Wimbush delights in her wit, and says there
is nothing so charming as to hear Mr. Paraday
draw it out. He is perpetually detailed for this
job, and he tells me it has a peculiarly exhausting
effect. Every one is beginning—at the end of two
days—to sidle obsequiously away from her, and
Mrs. Wimbush pushes him again and again into
the breach. None of the uses I have yet seen him
put to irritate me quite so much. He looks very
fagged, and has at last confessed to me that his
condition makes him uneasy—has even promised
me that he will go straight home instead of returning to his final engagements in town. Last
night I had some talk with him about going to-
day, cutting his visit short ; so sure am I that he
will be better as soon as he is shut up in his light-
house. He told me that this is what he would

like to do ; reminding me, however, that the first
lesson of his greatness has been precisely that he
can't do what he likes. Mrs. Wimbush would
never forgive him if he should leave her before
the princess has received the last hand. When I
say that a violent rupture with our hostess would
be the best thing in the world for him, he gives
me to understand that if his reason assents to the
proposition his courage hangs wofully back. He
makes no secret of being mortally afraid of her,
and when I ask what harm she can do him that
she hasn't already done he simply repeats : 'I'm
afraid, I'm afraid ! Don't enquire too closely,' he
said last night ; ' only believe that I feel a sort of
terror. It's strange, when she's so kind ! At any
rate, I would as soon overturn that piece of priceless Sèvres as tell her that I must go before my
date.' It sounds dreadfully weak, but he has
some reason, and he pays for his imagination,
which puts him (I should hate it) in the place of
others and makes him feel, even against himself,
their feelings, their appetites, their motives. It's
indeed inveterately against himself that he makes
his imagination act. What a pity he has such a
lot of it ! He's too beastly intelligent. Besides,
the famous reading is still to come off, and it has
been postponed a day, to allow Guy Walsingham to arrive. It appears that this eminent
lady is staying at a house a few miles off, which
means of course that Mrs. Wimbush has forci-
bly annexed her. She's to come over in a day

or two—Mrs. Wimbush wants her to hear Mr. Paraday.

"To-day's wet and cold, and several of the company, at the invitation of the duke, have driven over to luncheon at Bigwood. I saw poor Paraday wedge himself, by command, into the little supplementary seat of a brougham in which the Princess and our hostess were already ensconced. If the front glass isn't open on his dear old back, perhaps he'll survive. Bigwood, I believe, is very grand and frigid, all marble and precedence, and I wish him well out of the adventure. I can't tell you how much more and more *your* attitude to him, in the midst of all this, shines out by contrast. I never willingly talk to these people about him, but see what a comfort I find it to scribble to you! I appreciate it—it keeps me warm; there are no fires in the house. Mrs. Wimbush goes by the calendar, the temperature goes by the weather, the weather goes by God knows what, and the princess is easily heated. I have nothing but my acrimony to warm me, and have been out under an umbrella to restore my circulation. Coming in an hour ago, I found Lady Augusta Minch rummaging about the hall. When I asked her what she was looking for, she said she had mislaid something that Mr. Paraday had lent her. I ascertained in a moment that the article in question is a manuscript, and I have a foreboding that it's the noble morsel he read me six weeks ago. When I expressed my surprise that he should have bandied about any thing so precious (I happen to know it's his only copy—in the most beautiful hand in all the world) Lady Augusta confessed to me that she had not had it from himself, but from Mrs. Wimbush, who had wished to give her a glimpse of it as a salve for her not being able to stay and hear it read.

"'Is that the piece he's to read,' I asked, 'when Guy Walsingham arrives?'

"'It's not for Guy Walsingham they're waiting now, it's for Dora Forbes,' Lady Augusta said. 'She's coming, I believe, early to-morrow. Meanwhile, Mrs. Wimbush has found out about *him*, and is actively wiring to him. She says he also must hear him.'

"'You bewilder me a little,' I replied; 'in the age we live in one gets lost among the genders and the pronouns. The clear thing is that Mrs. Wimbush doesn't guard such a treasure as jealously as she might.'

"'Poor dear, she has the princess to guard! Mr. Paraday lent her the manuscript to look over.'

"'Did she speak as if it were the morning paper?'

"Lady Augusta stared—my irony was lost upon her. 'She didn't have time, so she gave me a chance first; because, unfortunately, I go to-morrow to Bigwood.'

"'And your chance has only proved a chance to lose it?'

"'I haven't lost it. I remember now—it was very stupid of me to have forgotten. I told my

maid to give it to Lord Dorimont, or at least to
his man.'

" ' And Lord Dorimont went away directly after
luncheon.'

" ' Of course he gave it back to my maid, or else
his man did,' said Lady Augusta.   'I dare say it's
all right.'

" The conscience of these people is like a.summer
sea.   They haven't time to ' look over ' a priceless
composition ; they've only time to kick it about
the house.   I suggested that the ' man,' fired with
a noble emulation, had perhaps kept the work for
his own perusal ; and her ladyship wanted to
know whether, if the thing didn't turn up again
in time for the session appointed by our hostess,
the author wouldn't have something else to read
that would do just as well.   Their questions are
too delightful !   I declared to Lady Augusta
briefly that nothing in the world can ever do so
well as the thing that does best, and at this she
looked a little confused and scared.   But I added
that if the manuscript had gone astray, our little
circle would have the less of an effort of attention
to make.   The piece in question was very long ; it
would keep them three hours.

" ' Three hours !   Oh, the princess will get up ! '
said Lady Augusta.

" ' I thought she was Mr. Paraday's greatest
admirer.'

" ' I dare say she is—she's so awfully clever.   But
what's the use of being a princess——'

4

" 'If you can't dissemble your love?' I asked,
as Lady Augusta was vague. She said, at any
rate, that she would question her maid ; and I am
hoping that when I go down to dinner I shall find
the manuscript has been recovered."

X

"It has not been recovered," I wrote early the
next day, "and I am moreover much troubled
about our friend. He came back from Bigwood
with a chill, and, being allowed to have a fire in his
room, lay down a while before dinner. I tried to
send him to bed, and indeed thought I had put him
in the way of it ; but after I had gone to dress
Mrs. Wimbush came up to see him, with the inevitable result that when I returned I found him
under arms and flushed and feverish, though decorated with the rare flower she had brought him
for his buttonhole. He came down to dinner, but
Lady Augusta Minch was very shy of him. To-
day he's in great pain, and the advent of *ces dames*
—I mean of Guy Walsingham and Dora Forbes—
doesn't at all console me. It does Mrs. Wimbush,
however, for she has consented to his remaining in
bed, so that he may be all right to-morrow for the
listening circle. Guy Walsingham is already on
the scene, and the doctor for Paraday also arrived
early. I haven't yet seen the author of ' Obses-

sions,' but of course I've had a moment by myself
with the doctor. I tried to get him to say that
our invalid must go straight home—I mean to-morrow or next day ; but he quite refuses to talk
about the future. Absolute quiet and warmth and
the regular administration of an important remedy
are the points he mainly insists on. He returns
this afternoon, and I'm to be back to see the patient
at one o'clock, when he next takes his medicine.
It consoles me a little that he certainly won't be able
to read—an exertion he was already more than unfit
for. Lady Augusta went off after breakfast, assur-
ing me that her first care would be to follow up the
lost manuscript. I can see she thinks me a shocking busybody and doesn't understand my alarm,
but she will do what she can, for she's a good-
natured woman. 'So are they all honorable men.'
That was precisely what made her give the thing
to Lord Dorimont and made Lord Dorimont bag
it. What use *he* has for it, God only knows ! I
have the worst forebodings, but somehow I'm
strangely without passion—desperately calm. As
I consider the unconscious, the well-meaning rav-
ages of our appreciative circle, I bow my head in
submission to some great natural, some universal
accident ; I'm rendered almost indifferent, in fact
quite gay (ha-ha !) by the sense of immitigable
fate. Lady Augusta promises me to trace the
precious object and let me have it, through the
post, by the time Paraday is well enough to play
his part with it. The last evidence is that her

maid did give it to his lordship's valet. One
would think it was some thrilling number of *The
Family Budget*. Mrs. Wimbush, who is aware of
the accident, is much less agitated by it than she
would doubtless be were she not for the hour
inevitably engrossed with Guy Walsingham."

Later in the day I informed my correspondent,
for whom indeed I kept a sort of diary of the situation, that I had made the acquaintance of this
celebrity, and that she was a pretty little girl who
wore her hair in what used to be called a crop.
She looked so juvenile and so innocent that if, as
Mr. Morrow had announced, she was resigned to
the larger latitude, her superiority to prejudice must
have come to her early. I spent most of the day
hovering about Neil Paraday's room, but it was
communicated to me from below that Guy Walsingham, at Prestidge, was a success. Toward evening
I became conscious somehow that her superiority
was contagious, and by the time the company
separated for the night I was sure that the larger
latitude had been generally accepted. I thought
of Dora Forbes, and felt that he had no time to
lose. Before dinner I received a telegram from
Lady Augusta Minch. "Lord Dorimont thinks
he must have left bundle in train--enquire." How
could I enquire--if I was to take the word as
command? I was too worried, and now too alarmed
about Neil Paraday. The doctor came back, and
it was an immense satisfaction to me to feel that

he was wise and interested. He was proud of being called to so distinguished a patient, but he admitted to me that night that my friend was gravely ill. It was really a relapse, a recrudescence of his old malady. There could be no question of moving him : we must at any rate see first, on the spot, what turn his condition would take. Meanwhile, on the morrow, he was to have a nurse. On the morrow the dear man was easier, and my spirits rose to such cheerfulness that I could almost laugh over Lady Augusta's second telegram : " Lord Dorimont's servant been to station—nothing found. Push enquiries." I did laugh, I am sure, as I remembered this to be the mystic scroll I had scarcely allowed poor Mr. Morrow to point his umbrella at. Fool that I had been ! The thirty-seven influential journals wouldn't have destroyed it, they would only have printed it. Of course I said nothing to Paraday.

When the nurse arrived she turned me out of the room, on which I went down stairs. I should premise that at breakfast the news that our brilliant friend was doing well excited universal complacency, and the princess graciously remarked that he was only to be commiserated for missing the society of Miss Collop. Mrs. Wimbush, whose social gift never shone brighter than in the dry decorum with which she accepted this fizzle in her fireworks, mentioned to me that Guy Walsingham had made a very favorable impression on her Imperial Highness. Indeed I think every one did so, and that, like the money-market or the national honor, her Imperial Highness was constitutionally sensitive. There was a certain gladness, a perceptible bustle in the air, however, which I thought slightly anomalous in a house where a great author lay critically ill. "*Le roy est mort—vive le roy!*" I was reminded that another great author had already stepped into his shoes. When I came down again after the nurse had taken possession I found a strange gentleman hanging about the hall and pacing to and fro by the closed door of the drawing-room. This personage was florid and bald; he had a big red mustache and wore showy knickerbockers—characteristics all that fitted into my conception of the identity of Dora Forbes. In a moment I saw what had happened: the author of "The Other Way Round" had just alighted at the portals of Prestidge, but had suffered a scruple to restrain him from penetrating further. I recognized his scruple when, pausing to listen at his gesture of caution, I heard a shrill voice lifted in a sort of rhythmic, uncanny chant. The famous reading had begun, only it was the author of "Obsessions" who now furnished the sacrifice. The new visitor whispered to me that he judged something was going on that he oughtn't to interrupt.

"Miss Collop arrived last night," I smiled, "and the princess has a thirst for the *inédit.*"

Dora Forbes lifted his bushy brows, "Miss Collop?"

"Guy Walsingham, your distinguished *confrère*
—or shall I say your formidable rival?"

"Oh!" growled Dora Forbes. Then he added:
"Shall I spoil it, if I go in?"

"I should think nothing could spoil it!" I
ambiguously laughed.

Dora Forbes evidently felt the dilemma; he
gave an irritated crook to his mustache. "*Shall*
I go in?" he presently asked.

We looked at each other hard a moment; then
I expressed something bitter that was in me, expressed it in an infernal "Do!" After this I got
out into the air, but not so fast as not to hear,
when the door of the drawing-room opened, the
disconcerted drop of Miss Collop's public manner:
she must have been in the midst of the larger latitude. Producing with extreme rapidity, Guy
Walsingham has just published a work in which
amiable people who are not initiated have been
pained to see the genius of a sister-novelist held
up to unmistakable ridicule; so fresh an exhibition does it seem to them of the dreadful way
men have always treated women. Dora Forbes,
it is true, at the present hour, is immensely
pushed by Mrs. Wimbush, and has sat for his portrait to the young artist she protects, sat for it
not only in oils, but in monumental alabaster.

What happened at Prestidge later in the day
is of course contemporary history. If the inter-
ruption I had whimsically sanctioned was almost
a scandal, what is to be said of that general dis-

persal of the company which, under the doctor's
rule, began to take place in the evening ! His rule
was soothing to behold, small comfort as I was to
have at the end. He decreed in the interest of
his patient an absolutely soundless house and a
consequent break-up of the party. Little country
practitioner as he was, he literally packed off
the princess. She departed as promptly as if a
revolution had broken out, and Guy Walsingham
emigrated with her. I was kindly permitted to
remain, and this was not denied even to Mrs.
Wimbush. The privilege was withheld indeed
from Dora Forbes ; so Mrs. Wimbush kept her
latest capture temporarily concealed. This was so
little, however, her usual way of dealing with her
eminent friends that a couple of days of it exhausted her patience, and she went up to town with
him in great publicity. The sudden turn for the
worse her afflicted guest had, after a brief improvement, taken on the third night raised an obstacle
to her seeing him before her retreat ; a fortunate
circumstance doubtless, for she was fundamentally disappointed in him. This was not the kind
of performance for which she had invited him to
Prestidge, or invited the princess. Let me hasten
to add that none of the generous acts which have
characterized her patronage of intellectual and other
merit have done so much for her reputation as her
lending Neil Paraday the most beautiful of her
numerous homes to die in. He took advantage to
the utmost of the singular favor. Day by day I

saw him sink, and I roamed alone about the empty terraces and gardens. His wife never camè near him, but I scarcely noticed it ; as I paced there with rage in my heart I was too full of another wrong. In the event of his death it would fall to me perhaps to bring out in some charming form, with notes, with the tenderest editorial care, that precious heritage of his written project. But where *was* the precious heritage, and were both the author and the book to be snatched from us ? Lady Augusta wrote me that she had done all she could, and that poor Lord Dorimont, who had really been worried to death, was extremely sorry. I couldn't have the matter out with Mrs. Wimbush, for I didn't want to be taunted by her with desiring to aggrandize myself by a public connection with Mr. Paraday's sweepings. She had signified her willingness to meet the expense of all advertising, as indeed she was always ready to do. The last night of the horrible series, the night before he died, I put my ear closer to his pillow.

"That thing I read you that morning, you know."

" In your garden that dreadful day ? Yes ! "

" Won't it do as it is ! "

" It would have been a glorious book."

" It *is* a glorious book," Neil Paraday murmured. " Print it as it stands—beautifully."

" Beautifully ! " I passionately promised.

It may be imagined whether, now that he is gone, the promise seems to me less sacred. I am convinced that if such pages had appeared in his life-time the Abbey would hold him to-day. I have kept the advertising in my own hands, but the manuscript has not been recovered. It is impossible, and at any rate intolerable, to suppose it can have been wantonly destroyed. Perhaps some hazard of a blind hand, some brutal ignorance, has lighted kitchen fires with it. Every stupid and hideous accident haunts my meditations. My undiscourageable search for the lost treasure would make a long chapter. Fortunately, I have a devoted associate in the person of a young lady who has every day a fresh indignation and a fresh idea, and who maintains with intensity that the prize will still turn up. Sometimes I believe her, but I have quite ceased to believe myself. The only thing for us, at all events, is to go on seeking and hoping together ; and we should be closely united by this firm tie even were we not at present by another.

THE COXON FUND

I

"THEY'VE got him for life!" I said to myself
that evening on my way back to the station; but
later, alone in the compartment (from Wimbledon
to Waterloo, before the glory of the District
Railway), I amended this declaration in the light
of the sense that my friends would probably after
all not enjoy a monopoly of Mr. Saltram. I won't
pretend to have taken his vast measure on that
first occasion, but I think I had achieved a glimpse
of what the privilege of his acquaintance might
mean for many persons in the way of charges accepted. He had been a great experience, and it
was this, perhaps, that had put me into the frame
of foreseeing how we should all, sooner or later,
have the honor of dealing with him as a whole.
Whatever impression I then received of the amount
of this total, I had a full enough vision of the
patience of the Mullvilles. He was staying with
them all the winter: Adelaide dropped it in a tone
which drew the sting from the temporary. These
excellent people might indeed have been content
to give the circle of hospitality a diameter of six
months; but if they didn't say that he was stay-

ing for the summer as well, it was only because
this was more than they ventured to hope. I remember that at dinner that evening he wore slip-
pers, new and predominantly purple, of some queer
carpet-stuff ; but the Mulvilles were still in the
stage of supposing that he might be snatched from
them by higher bidders. At a later time they
grew, poor dears, to fear no snatching ; but theirs
was a fidelity which needed no help from compe-
tition to make them proud. Wonderful indeed as,
when all was said, you inevitably pronounced Frank
Saltram, it was not to be overlooked that the Kent
Mulvilles were in their way still more extraordinary : as striking an instance as could easily be
encountered of the familiar truth that remarkable
men find remarkable conveniences.

They had sent for me from Wimbledon to come
out and dine, and there had been an implication in
Adelaide's note (judged by her notes alone she
might have been thought silly) that it was a case
in which something momentous was to be determined or done. I had never known them not to
be in a "state" about somebody, and I dare say I
tried to be droll on this point in accepting their invitation. On finding myself in the presence of their
latest revelation I had not at first felt irreverence
droop ; and, thank Heaven, I have never been absolutely deprived of that alternative in Mr. Saltram's
company. I saw, however (I hasten to declare it),
that, compared to this specimen, their other phœ-
nixes had been birds of inconsiderable feather, and

I afterward took credit to myself for not having, even in primal bewilderments, made a mistake about the essence of the man. He had an incomparable gift; I never was blind to it—it dazzles me at present. It dazzles me perhaps even more in remembrance than in fact, for I'm not unaware that for a subject so magnificent the imagination goes to some expense, inserting a jewel here and there or giving a twist to a plume. How the art of portraiture would rejoice in this figure if the art of portraiture had only the canvas! Nature, in truth, had largely rounded it, and if Memory, hovering about it, sometimes holds her breath, this is because the voice that comes back was really golden.

Though the great man was an inmate and didn't dress, he kept dinner on this occasion waiting, and the first words he uttered on coming into the room were a triumphant announcement to Mulville that he had found out something. Not catching the allusion, and gaping doubtless a little at his face, I privately asked Adelaide what he had found out. I shall never forget the look she gave me as she replied, "Every thing!" She really believed it. At that moment, at any rate, he had found out that the mercy of the Mulvilles was infinite. He had previously of course discovered, as I had myself for that matter, that their dinners were *soignés*. Let me not indeed, in saying this, neglect to declare that I shall falsify my counterfeit if I seem to hint that there was in his nature any ounce of

calculation.   He took whatever came, but he never
plotted for it, and no man who was so much of an
absorbent can ever have been so little of a parasite.
He had a system of the universe, but he had no
system of sponging—that was quite hand-to-mouth.
He had fine, gross, easy senses, but it was not his
good-natured appetite that wrought confusion.   If
he had loved us for our dinners we could have
paid with our dinners, and it would have been a
great economy of finer matter.   I make free in
these connections with the plural possessive because,
if I was never able to do what the Mulvilles did,
and people with still bigger houses and simpler
charities, I met, first and last, every demand of
reflection, of emotion—particularly, perhaps, those
of gratitude and of resentment.   No one, I think,
paid the tribute of giving him up so often, and, if
it's rendering honor to borrow wisdom, I have a
right to talk of my sacrifices.   He yielded lessons
as the sea yields fish—I lived for a while on this
diet.   Sometimes it almost appeared to me that his
massive, monstrous failure—if failure, after all, it
was—had been intended for my private recreation.
He fairly pampered my curiosity ; but the history
of that experience would take me too far.   This is
not the large canvas I just now spoke of, and I
would not have approached him with my present
hand had it been a question of all the features.
Frank Saltram's features, for artistic purposes, are
verily the anecdotes that are to be gathered.
Their name is legion, and this is only one, of which

the interest is that it concerns even more closely several other persons. Such episodes, as one looks back, are the little dramas that made up the innumerable facets of the big drama—which is yet to be reported.

II

It is furthermore remarkable that though the two stories are distinct—my own, as it were, and this other—they equally began, in a manner, the first night of my acquaintance with Frank Saltram, the night I came back from Wimbledon so agitated with a new sense of life that, in London, for the very thrill of it, I could only walk home. Walking and swinging my stick, I overtook, at Buckingham Gate, George Gravener, and George Gravener's story may be said to have begun with my making him, as our paths lay together, come home with me for a talk. I duly remember, let me parenthesize, that it was still more that of another person, and also that several years were to elapse before it was to extend to a second chapter. I had much to say to him, none the less, about my visit to the Mulvilles, whom he more indifferently knew, and I was at any rate so amusing that, for long afterward, he never encountered me without asking for news of the old man of the sea. I hadn't said Mr. Saltram was old, and it was to be seen that he was of an age to outweather George Gravener. I had at that time a lodging in Ebury Street, and Gravener was staying at his brother's empty house in Eaton Square. At Cambridge, five years before, even in our devastating set, his intellectual power had seemed to me almost awful. Some one had once asked me privately, with blanched cheeks, what it was then that, after all, such a mind as that left standing. "It leaves itself!" I could recollect devoutly replying. I could smile at present at this reminiscence, for even before we got to Ebury Street I was struck with the fact that, save in the sense of being well set up on his legs, George Gravener had actually ceased to tower. The universe he laid low had somehow bloomed again— the usual eminences were visible. I wondered whether he had lost his humor, or only, dreadful thought! had never had any—not even when I had fancied him most Aristophanesque. What was the need of appealing to laughter, however, I could enviously enquire, where you might appeal so confidently to measurement? Mr. Saltram's queer figure, his thick nose and hanging lip, were fresh to me; in the light of my old friend's fine cold symmetry they presented mere success in amusing as the refuge of conscious ugliness. Already, at hungry twenty-six, Gravener looked as blank and parliamentary as if he were fifty and popular. In my scrap of a residence (he had a worldling's eye for its futile conveniencies, but never a comrade's joke) I sounded Frank Saltram in his ears ; a circumstance I mention in order to note that even then I was surprised at his impatience of my enlivenment. As he had never before heard of the personage, it took indeed the form of impatience of the preposterous Mulvilles, his relation to whom, like mine, had had its origin in an early, a childish intimacy with the young Adelaide, the fruit of multiplied ties in the previous generation. When she married Kent Mulville, who was older than Gravener and I and much more amiable, I gained a friend, but Gravener practically lost one. We were affected in different ways by the form taken by what he called their deplorable social action— the form (the term was also his) of nasty, second-rate gush. I may have held in my *for intérieur* that the good people at Wimbledon were beautiful fools, but when he sniffed at them I couldn't help taking the opposite line, for I already felt that, even should we happen to agree, it would always be for reasons that differed. It came home to me that he was admirably British as, without so much as a sociable sneer at my bookbinder, he turned away from the serried rows of my little French library.

"Of course I've never seen the fellow, but it's clear enough he's a humbug."

"Clear 'enough' is just what it isn't," I replied ; "if it only were !" That ejaculation on my part must have been the beginning of what was to be later a long ache for final, frivolous rest. Gravener was profound enough to remark after a moment that in the first place he couldn't be any thing but

5

a dissenter, and when I answered that the very note of his fascination was his extraordinary speculative breadth, my friend retorted that there was no cad like your cultivated cad, and that I might depend upon discovering, since I had had the levity not already to have enquired, that my shining light proceeded, a generation back, from a Methodist cheesemonger. I confess I was struck with his insistence, and I said, after reflection : " It may be —I admit it may be ; but why on earth are you so sure ? "—asking the question mainly to lay him the trap of saying that it was because the poor man didn't dress for dinner. He took an instant to circumvent my trap and came blandly out the other side.

" Because the Kent Mulvilles have invented him. They've an infallible hand for frauds. All their geese are swans. They were born to be duped, they like it, they cry for it, they don't know any thing from any thing, and they disgust one (luckily perhaps !) with Christian charity." His vehemence was doubtless an accident, but it might have been a strange foreknowledge. I forget what protest I dropped ; it was at any rate something which led him to go on after a moment : " I only ask one thing—it's perfectly simple. Is a man, in a given case, a real gentleman ? "

" A real gentleman, my dear fellow—that's so soon said ! "

"Not so soon when he isn't ! If they've got hold of one this time he must be a great rascal ! "

"I might feel injured," I answered, "if I didn't reflect that they don't rave about *me*."

"Don't be too sure! I'll grant that he's a gentleman," Gravener presently added, "if you'll admit that he's a scamp."

"I don't know which to admire most, your logic or your benevolence."

My friend colored at this, but he didn't change the subject. "Where did they pick him up?"

"I think they were struck with something he had published."

"I can fancy the dreary thing!"

"I believe they found out he had all sorts of worries and difficulties."

"That, of course, was not to be endured, and they jumped at the privilege of paying his debts!"

I replied that I knew nothing about his debts, and I reminded my visitor that though the dear Mulvilles were angels they were neither idiots nor millionnaires. What they mainly aimed at was reuniting Mr. Saltram to his wife.

"I was expecting to hear that he has basely abandoned her," Gravener went on, at this, "and I'm too glad you don't disappoint me."

I tried to recall exactly what Mrs. Mulville had told me. "He didn't leave her—no. It's she who has left him."

"Left him to *us*?" Gravener asked. "The monster—many thanks! I decline to take him."

"You'll hear more about him in spite of yourself. I can't, no, I really can't resist the impres-

sion that he's a big man." I was already learning
—to my shame perhaps be it said—just the tone
that my old friend least liked.

"It's doubtless only a trifle," he returned, "but
you haven't happened to mention what his reputation's to rest on."

"Why, on what I began by boring you with—
his extraordinary mind."

"As exhibited in his writings?"

"Possibly in his writings, but certainly in his
talk, which is far and away the richest I ever
listened to."

"And what is it all about?"

"My dear fellow, don't ask me! About every
thing!" I pursued, reminding myself of poor
Adelaide. "About his ideas of things," I then
more charitably added. "You must have heard
him to know what I mean—it's unlike any thing
that ever *was* heard." I colored, I admit, I over-
charged a little, for such a picture was an anticipa-
tion of Saltram's later development and still more
of my fuller acquaintance with him. However, I
really expressed, a little lyrically perhaps, my
actual imagination of him when I proceeded to
declare that, in a cloud of tradition, of legend, he
might very well go down to posterity as the greatest of all great talkers. Before we parted George
Gravener demanded why such a row should be
madé about a chatterbox the more, and why he
should be pampered and pensioned. The greater
the wind-bag, the greater the calamity. Out of

proportion to every thing else on earth had come to be this wagging of the tongue. We were drenched with talk—our wretched age was dying of it. I differed from him here sincerely, only going so far as to concede, and gladly, that we were drenched with sound. It was not, however, the mere speakers who were killing us—it was the mere stammerers. Fine talk was as rare as it was refreshing—the gift of the gods themselves, the one starry spangle on the ragged cloak of humanity. How many men were there who rose to this privilege, of how many masters of conversation could he boast the acquaintance? Dying of talk? why, we were dying of the lack of it! Bad writing wasn't talk, as many people seemed to think, and even good wasn't always to be compared to it. From the best talk, indeed, the best writing had something to learn. I fancifully added that we too should peradventure be gilded by the legend, should be pointed at for having listened, for having actually heard. Gravener, who had glanced at his watch and discovered it was midnight, found to all this a response beautifully characteristic of him.

"There is one little fact to be borne in mind in the presence equally of the best talk and of the worst." He looked, in saying this, as if he meant so much that I thought he could only mean once more that neither of them mattered if a man wasn't a real gentleman. Perhaps it was what he did mean; he deprived me, however, of the exultation of being right by putting the truth in a slightly different way. "The only thing that really counts for one's estimate of a person is his conduct." He had his watch still in his hand, and I reproached him with unfair play in having ascertained before-hand that it was now the hour at which I always gave in. My pleasantry so far failed to mollify him that he promptly added that to the rule he had just enunciated there was absolutely no exception.

"None whatever?"

"None whatever!"

"Trust me, then, to try to be good at any price!" I laughed as I went with him to the door. "I declare I will be, if I have to be horrible!"

III

If that first night was one of the liveliest, or at any rate was the freshest, of my exaltations, there was another, four years later, that was one of my great discomposures. Repetition, I well knew by this time, was the secret of Saltram's power to alienate, and of course one would never have seen him at his finest if one hadn't seen him in his remorses. They set in mainly at this season, and were magnificent, orchestral. I was perfectly aware that something of the sort was now due; but none the less, in our arduous attempt to set him on his feet as a lecturer, it was impossible not

to feel that two failures were a large order, as we
said, for a short course of five. This was the
second time, and it was past nine o'clock; the
audience, a muster unprecedented and really
encouraging, had fortunately the attitude of
blandness that might have been looked for in persons whom the promise (if I am not mistaken) of
an Analysis of Primary Ideas had drawn to the
neighborhood of Upper Baker Street. There
was in those days in that region a petty lecture-
hall to be secured on terms as moderate as the
funds left at our disposal by the irrepressible question of the maintenance of five small Saltrams (I
include the mother) and one large one. By the
time the Saltrams, of different sizes, were all maintained, we had pretty well poured out the oil that
might have lubricated the machinery for enabling
the most original of men to appear to maintain
them.

It was I, the other time, who had been forced
into the breach, standing up there for an odious
lamplit moment to explain to half a dozen thin
benches, where the earnest brows were virtuously
void of any thing so cynical as a suspicion, that
we couldn't put so much as a finger on Mr. Saltram.
There was nothing to plead but that our scouts
had been out from the early hours, and that we
were afraid that on one of his walks abroad—he
took one, for meditation, whenever he was to
address such a company—some accident had dis-
abled or delayed him. The meditative walks were

a fiction, for he never, that any one could discover, prepared any thing but a magnificent prospectus ; so that his circulars and programmes, of which I possess an almost complete collection, are the solemn ghosts of generations never born. I put the case, as it seemed to me, at the best ; but I admit I had been angry, and Kent Mulville was shocked at my want of public optimism. This time, therefore, I left the excuses to his more prac-tised patience, only relieving myself in response to a direct appeal from a young lady, next whom, in the hall, I found myself sitting. My position was an accident, but if it had been calculated the reason would scarcely have eluded an observer of the fact that no one else in the room had an approach to an appearance. Our philosopher's "tail" was deplorably limp. This visitor was the only person who looked at her ease, who had come a little in the spirit of adventure. She seemed to carry amusement in her handsome young head, and her presence quite gave me the sense of a sudden extension of Saltram's sphere of influence. He was doing better than we hoped, and he had chosen such an occasion, of all occasions, to suc-cumb to Heaven knew which of his infirmities. The young lady produced an impression of auburn hair and black velvet, and had on her other hand a companion of obscurer type, presumably a wait-ing-maid. She herself might perhaps have been a foreign countess, and before she spoke to me I had beguiled our sorry interval by thinking that she brought vaguely back the first page of some novel of Mme. Sand. It didn't make her more fathomable to perceive in a few minutes that she could only be an American ; it simply engendered depressing reflections as to the possible check to contributions from Boston. She asked me if, as a person apparently more initiated, I would recommend further waiting, and I replied that, if she considered I was on my honor, I would privately deprecate it. Perhaps she didn't ; at any rate something passed between us that led us to talk until she became aware that we were almost the only people left. I presently discovered that she knew Mrs. Saltram, and this explained in a manner the miracle. The brotherhood of the friends of the husband was as nothing to the brotherhood, or perhaps I should say the sisterhood, of the friends of the wife. Like the Kent Mulvilles, I belonged to both fraternities, and, even better than they, I think I had sounded the abyss of Mrs. Saltram's wrongs. She bored me to extinction, and I knew but too well how she had bored her husband ; but she had those who stood by her, the most efficient of whom were indeed the handful of poor Saltram's backers. They did her liberal justice, whereas her mere patrons and partisans had nothing but hatred for our philosopher. I am bound to say it was we, however,—we of both camps, as it were,—who had always done most for her.

I thought my young lady looked rich—I scarcely knew why ; and I hoped she had put her hand in

her pocket. But I soon discovered that she was
not a fine fanatic—she was only a generous, irre-
sponsible enquirer. She had come to England to
see her aunt, and it was at her aunt's she had met
the dreary lady we had all so much on our mind.
I saw she would help to pass the time when she
observed that it was a pity this lady wasn't intrin-
sically more interesting. That was refreshing,
for it was an article of faith in Mrs. Saltram's
circle—at least among those who scorned to know
her horrid husband—that she was attractive on
her merits. She was really a very common person, as Saltram himself would have been if he
hadn't been a prodigy. The question of vulgarity
had no application to him, but it was a measure
that his wife kept challenging you to apply. I
hasten to add that the consequences of your doing
so were no sufficient reason for his having left her
to starve. "He doesn't seem to have much force
of character," said my young lady; at which
I laughed out so loud that my departing friends
looked back at me over their shoulders as if I were
making a joke of their discomfiture. My joke
probably cost Saltram a subscription or two, but
it helped me on with my interlocutress. "She
says he drinks like a fish," she sociably continued,
"and yet she admits that his mind is wonderfully
clear." It was amusing to converse with a pretty
girl who could talk of the clearness of Saltram's
mind. I expected her next to say that she had
been assured he was awfully clever. I tried to tell

her—I had it almost on my conscience—what was the proper way to regard him ; an effort attended perhaps more than ever on this occasion with the usual effect of my feeling that I wasn't after all very sure of it. She had come to-night out of high curiosity—she had wanted to find out this proper way for herself. She had read some of his papers and hadn't understood them ; but it was at home, at her aunt's, that her curiosity had been kindled—kindled mainly by his wife's remarkable stories of his want of virtue. "I suppose they ought to have kept me away," my companion dropped, " and I suppose they would have done so, if I hadn't somehow got an idea that he's fascinating. In fact Mrs. Saltram herself says he is."

" So you came to see where the fascination resides ? Well, you've seen ! "

My young lady raised her fine eyebrows. " Do you mean in his bad faith ? "

" In the extraordinary effects of it ; his possession, that is, of some quality or other that condemns us in advance to forgive him the humiliation, as I may call it, to which he has subjected us."

" The humiliation ? "

" Why, mine, for instance, as one of his guarantors, before you as the purchaser of a ticket."

" You don't look humiliated a bit, and if you did I should let you off, disappointed as I am ; for the mysterious quality you speak of is just the quality I came to see."

" Oh, you can't ' see ' it ! " I exclaimed.

" How, then, do you get at it ? "

" You don't ! You mustn't suppose he's good-looking," I added.

" Why, his wife says he's lovely ! "

My hilarity may have struck my interlocutress as excessive, but I confess it broke out afresh. Had she acted only in obedience to this singular plea, so characteristic, on Mrs. Saltram's part, of what was irritating in the narrowness of that lady's point of view ? " Mrs. Saltram," I explained, " undervalues him where he is strongest, so that, to make up for it, perhaps, she overpraises him where he's weak. He's not, assuredly, superficially attractive ; he's middle-aged, fat, featureless, save for his great eyes."

" Yes, his great eyes," said my young lady attentively. She had evidently heard all about his great eyes—the *beaux yeux* for which alone we had really done it all.

" They're tragic and splendid—lights on a dangerous coast. But he moves badly and dresses worse, and altogether he's any thing but smart."

My companion appeared to reflect on this, and after a moment she enquired : " Do you call him a real gentleman ? "

I started slightly at the question, for I had a sense of recognizing it ; George Gravener, years before, that first flushed night, had put me face to face with it. It had embarrassed me then, but it didn't embarrass me now, for I had lived with it and overcome it and disposed of it. "A real gentleman ? Emphatically not ! "

My promptitude surprised her a little, but I quickly felt that it was not to Gravener I was now talking. "Do you say that because he's—what do you call it in England ?—of humble extraction ?"

"Not a bit. His father was a country schoolmaster and his mother the widow of a sexton, but that has nothing to do with it. I say it simply because I know him well."

"But isn't it an awful drawback ?"

"Awful—quite awful."

"I mean isn't it positively fatal ?"

"Fatal to what ? Not to his magnificent vitality."

Again there was a meditative moment. "And is his magnificent vitality the cause of his vices ?"

"Your questions are formidable, but I'm glad you put them. I was thinking of his noble intellect. His vices, as you say, have been much exaggerated : they consist mainly, after all, in one comprehensive defect."

"A want of will ? "

"A want of dignity."

"He doesn't recognize his obligations ?"

"On the contrary, he recognizes them with effusion, especially in public ; he smiles and bows and beckons across the street to them. But when they pass over he turns away, and he speedily loses them in the crowd. The recognition is purely spiritual—it isn't in the least social. So he leaves all his belongings to other people to take care of. He accepts favors, loans, sacrifices, with nothing more deterrent than an agony of shame. Fortunately we're a little faithful band, and we do what we can." I held my tongue about the natural children, engendered, to the number of three, in the wantonness of his youth. I only remarked that he did make efforts—often tremendous ones. "But the efforts," I said, "never come to much ; the only things that come to much are the abandonments, the surrenders."

"And how much do they come to ?"

"You're right to put it as if we had a big bill to pay, but, as I've told you before, your questions are rather terrible. They come, these mere exercises of genius, to a great sum total of poetry, of philosophy, a mighty mass of speculation, of notation. The genius is there, you see, to meet the surrender ; but there's no genius to support the defence."

"But what is there, after all, at his age, to show ?"

"In the way of achievement recognized and reputation established ?" I interrupted. "To 'show' if you will, there isn't much, for his writing, mostly, isn't as fine, isn't certainly as showy, as his talk. Moreover, two-thirds of his work are merely colossal projects and announcements. 'Showing' Frank Saltram is often a poor business ; we endeavored, you will have observed, to show him to-night ! However, if he *had* lectured, he would have lectured divinely. It would just have been his talk."

" And what would his talk just have been?"

I was conscious of some ineffectiveness as well perhaps as of a little impatience as I replied : " The exhibition of a splendid intellect." My young lady looked not quite satisfied at this, but as I was not prepared for another question I hastily pursued: " The sight of a great suspended, swinging crystal, huge, lucid, lustrous, a block of light, flashing back every impression of life and every possibility of thought !" This gave her something to think about till we had passed out to the dusky porch of the hall, in front of which the lamps of a quiet brougham were almost the only thing Saltram's treachery hadn't extinguished. I went with her to the door of her carriage, out of which she leaned a moment after she had thanked me and had taken her seat. Her smile, even in the darkness, was pretty. "I do want to see that crystal !"

" You've only to come to the next lecture."

" I go abroad in a day or two with my aunt."

" Wait over till next week," I suggested. "It's quite worth it."

She became grave. "Not unless he really comes !" At which the brougham started off, carrying her away too fast, fortunately for my manners, to allow me to exclaim "Ingratitude !"

IV

Mrs. Saltram made a great affair of her right to
be informed where her husband had been the second evening he failed to meet his audience. She
came to me to ascertain, but I couldn't satisfy her,
for in spite of my ingenuity I remained in ignorance. It was not till much later that I found this
had not been the case with Kent Mulville, whose
hope for the best never twirled his thumbs more
placidly than when he happened to know the
worst. He had known it on the occasion I speak
of—that is, immediately after. He was impenetrable then, but he ultimately confessed. What
he confessed was more than I shall venture to confess to-day. It was of course familiar to me that
Saltram was incapable of keeping the engagements
which, after their separation, he had entered into
with regard to his wife, a deeply wronged, justly
resentful, quite irreproachable and insufferable
person. She often appeared at my chambers to
talk over his lapses ; for if, as she declared, she had
washed her hands of him, she had carefully pre-
served the water of this ablution and she handed
it about for inspection. She had arts of her own
of exciting one's impatience, the most infallible of
which was perhaps her assumption that we were

kind to her because we liked her. In reality her
personal fall had been a sort of social rise, for
there had been a moment when, in our little con-
scientious circle, her desolation almost made her
the fashion. Her voice was grating and her children ugly ; moreover she hated the good Mulvilles, whom I more and more loved. They were
the people who, by doing most for her husband,
had in the long run done most for herself ; and the
warm confidence with which he had laid his length
upon them was a pressure gentle compared with
her stiffer persuadability. I am bound to say he
didn't criticise his benefactors, though practically
he got tired of them ; she, however, had the
highest standards about eleemosynary forms. She
offered the odd spectacle of a spirit puffed up by
dependence, and indeed it had introduced her to
some excellent society. She pitied me for not
knowing certain people who aided her, and whom
she doubtless patronized in turn for their luck in
not knowing me. I dare say I should have got on
with her better if she had had a ray of imagination—if it had occasionally seemed to occur to her
to regard Saltram's manifestations in any other
manner than as separate subjects of woe. They
were all flowers of his nature, pearls strung on an
endless thread ; but she had a stubborn little way
of challenging them one after the other, as if she
never suspected that he *had* a nature, such as it
was, or that deficiencies might be organic ; the
irritating effect of a mind incapable of a generali-

6

zation. One might doubtless have overdone the
idea that there was a general exemption for such
a man ; but, if this had happened, it would have
been through one's feeling that there could be
none for such a woman.

I recognized her superiority when I asked her
about the aunt of the disappointed young lady ; it
sounded like a sentence from a phrase-book. She
triumphed in what she told me, and she may have
triumphed still more in what she withheld. My
friend of the other evening, Miss Anvoy, had but
lately come to England ; Lady Coxon, the aunt,
had been established here for years in consequence
of her marriage with the late Sir Gregory of that
ilk. She had a house in the Regent's Park, a
bath-chair, and a fernery ; and above all she had
sympathy. Mrs. Saltram had made her acquaintance through mutual friends. This vagueness
caused me to feel how much I was out of it, and
how large an independent circle Mrs. Saltram had
at her command. I should have been glad to
know more about the disappointed young lady,
but I felt that I should know most by not depriving her of her advantage, as she might have mysterious means of depriving me of my knowledge.
For the present, moreover, this experience was
arrested, Lady Coxon having in fact gone abroad,
accompanied by her niece. The niece, besides
being immensely clever, was an heiress, Mrs. Saltram said ; the only daughter and the light of the
eyes of some great American merchant, a man,

over there, of endless indulgences and dollars. She had pretty clothes and pretty manners, and she had, what was prettier still, the great thing of all. The great thing of all for Mrs. Saltram was always sympathy, and she spoke as if, during the absence of these ladies, she might not know where to turn for it. A few months later indeed, when they had come back, her tone perceptibly changed; she alluded to them, on my leading her up to it, rather as to persons in her debt for favors received. What had happened I didn't know, but I saw it would take only a little more or a little less to make her speak of them as thankless subjects of social countenance—people for whom she had vainly tried to do something. I confess I saw that it would not be in a mere week or two that I should rid myself of the image of Ruth Anvoy, in whose very name, when I learned it, I found something secretly to like. I should probably neither see her nor hear of her again ; the knight's widow (he had been mayor of Clockborough) would pass away and the heiress would return to her inheritance. I gathered with surprise that she had not communicated to his wife the story of her attempt to hear Mr. Saltram, and I founded this reticence on the easy supposition that Mrs. Saltram had fatigued by over-pressure the spring of the sympathy of which she boasted. The girl at any rate would forget the small adventure, be distracted, take a husband ; besides which she would lack opportunity to repeat her experiment.

We clung to the idea of the brilliant course, delivered without an accident, that, as a lecturer,
would still make the paying public aware of our
great mind ; but the fact remained that in the
case of an inspiration so unequal there was treachery ; there was fallacy, at least, in the very conception of a series.   In our scrutiny of ways and
means we were inevitably subject to the old con-
vention of the synopsis, the syllabus—partly of
course not to lose the advantage of his grand free
hand in drawing up such things ; but, for myself,
I laughed at our playbills, even while I stickled
for them.   It was indeed amusing work to be
scrupulous for Frank Saltram, who also at
moments laughed about it, so far as the comfort of
a sigh so unstudied as to be cheerful might pass
for such a sound.   He admitted with a candor all
his own that he was in truth only to be depended
on in the Mulvilles' drawing-room.   "Yes," he
suggestively conceded, "it's there, I think, that I
am at my best ; quite late, when it gets toward
eleven—and if I've not been too much worried."
We all knew what too much worry meant ; it
meant too enslaved for the hour to the superstition
of sobriety.   On the Saturdays I used to bring my
portmanteau, so as not to have to think of eleven
o'clock trains.   I had a bold theory that as regards
this temple of talk and its altars of ˏcushioned
chintz, its pictures and its flowers, its large fire-
side and clear lamplight, we might really arrive at
something if the Mulvilles would only charge **for**

admission. But here it was that the Mulvilles
shamelessly broke down ; as there is a flaw in
every perfection, this was the inexpugnable refuge
of their egotism. They declined to make their
saloon a market, so that Saltram's golden words
continued to be the only coin that rang there. It
can have happened to no man, however, to be paid
a greater price than such an enchanted hush as
surrounded him on his greatest nights. The most
profane, on these occasions, felt a presence ; all
minor eloquence grew dumb. Adelaide Mulville,
for the pride of her hospitality, anxiously watched
the door or stealthily poked the fire. I used to
call it the music-room, for we had anticipated
Bayreuth. The very gates of the kingdom of
light seemed to open, and the horizon of thought
to flash with the beauty of a sunrise at sea.

In the consideration of ways and means, the sit-
tings of our little board, we were always conscious
of the creak of Mrs. Saltram's shoes. She hovered,
she interrupted, she almost presided ; the state of
affairs being mostly such as to supply her with
every incentive for enquiring what was to be done
next. It was the pressing pursuit of this knowledge that, in concatenations of omnibuses and
usually in very wet weather, led her so often to
my door. She thought us spiritless creatures with
editors and publishers ; but she carried matters to
no great effect when she personally pushed into
back-shops. She wanted all moneys to be paid to
herself ; they were otherwise liable to such strange

adventures. They trickled away into the desert, and they were mainly at best, alas! but a slender stream. The editors and the publishers were the last people to take this remarkable thinker at the valuation that has now pretty well come to be established. The former were half distraught between the desire to "cut" him and the difficulty of finding a crevice for their shears ; and when a volume on this or that portentous subject was proposed to the latter they suggested alternative titles which, as reported to our friend, brought into his face the noble blank melancholy that sometimes made it handsome. The title of an unwritten book didn't after all much matter, but some masterpiece of Saltram's may have died in his bosom of the shudder with which it was then convulsed. The ideal solution, failing the fee at Kent Mulville's door, would have been some system of subscription to projected treatises with their non-appearance provided for— provided for, I mean, by the indulgence of subscribers. The author's real misfortune was that subscribers were so wretchedly literal. When they tastelessly enquired why publication had not ensued, I was tempted to ask who in the world had ever been so published. Nature herself had brought him out in voluminous form, and the money was simply a deposit on borrowing the work.

V

I was doubtless often a nuisance to my friends in those years ; but there were sacrifices I declined to make, and I never passed the hat to George Gravener. I never forgot our little discussion in Ebury Street, and I think it stuck in my throat to have to make to him the admission I had made so easily to Miss Anvoy. It had cost me nothing to confide to this charming girl, but it would have cost me much to confide to the friend of my youth that the character of the "real gentleman" was not an attribute of the man I took such pains for. Was this because I had already generalized to the point of perceiving that women are really the unfastidious sex ? I knew at any rate that Gravener, already quite in view but still hungry and frugal, had, naturally enough, more ambition than charity. He had sharp aims for stray sovereigns, being in view most from the tall steeple of Clockborough. His immediate ambition was to wholly occupy the field of vision of that smokily-seeing city, and all his movements and postures were calculated for this angle. The movement of the hand to the pocket had thus to alternate gracefully with the posture of the hand on the heart. He talked to Clockborough, in short, only less beguilingly than

Frank Saltram talked to his electors; with the difference in our favor, however, that we had already voted and that our candidate had no antagonist but himself. He had more than once been at Wimbledon,—it was Mrs. Mulville's work, not mine,—and, by the time the claret was served, had seen the god descend. He took more pains to swing his censer than I had expected, but on our way back to town he forestalled any little triumph I might have been so artless as to express by the observation that such a man was—a hundred times!—a man to use and never a man to be used by. I remember that this neat remark humiliated me almost as much as if, virtually, in the fever of broken slumbers, I hadn't often made it myself. The difference was that on Gravener's part a force attached to it that could never attach to it on mine. He was able to use people—he had the machinery; and the irony of Saltram's being made showy at Clockborough came out to me when he said, as if he had no memory of our original talk and the idea were quite fresh to him, "I hate his type, you know, but I'll be hanged if I don't put some of those things in. I can find a place for them; we might even find a place for the fellow himself." I myself should have had some fear, not, I need scarcely say, for the "things" themselves, but for some other things very near them—in fine for the rest of my eloquence.

Later on I could see that the oracle of Wimbledon was not in this case so appropriate as he would have been had the politics of the gods only coincided more exactly with those of the party. There was a distinct moment when, without saying any thing more definite to me, Gravener entertained the idea of annexing Mr. Saltram. Such a project was delusive, for the discovery of analogies between his body of doctrine and that pressed from headquarters upon Clockborough—the bottling, in a word, of the air of those lungs for convenient public uncorking in corn-exchanges—was an experiment for which no one had the leisure. The only thing would have been to carry him massively about, paid, caged, clipped ; to turn him on for a particular occasion in a particular channel. Frank Saltram's channel, however, was essentially not calculable, and there was no knowing what disastrous floods might have ensued. For what there would have been to do *The Empire,* the great newspaper, was there to look to; but it was no new misfortune that there were delicate situations in which *The Empire* broke down. In fine, there was an instinctive apprehension that a clever young journalist commissioned to report upon Mr. Saltram might never come back from the errand. No one knew better than George Gravener that that was a time when prompt returns counted double. If he, therefore, found our friend an exasperating waste of orthodoxy, it was because he was, as he said, up in the clouds, not because he was down in the dust. He would have been a real enough gentleman, if he could have helped to put in a real gentleman.

Gravener's great objection to the actual member was that he was not one.

Lady Coxon had a fine old house, a house with "grounds," at Clockborough, which she had let; but after she returned from abroad I learned from Mrs. Saltram that the lease had fallen in and that she had gone down to resume possession. I could see the faded red livery, the big square shoulders, the high-walled garden of this decent abode. As the rumble of dissolution grew louder the suitor would have pressed his suit, and I found myself hoping that the politics of the late mayor's widow would not be such as to enjoin upon her to ask him to dinner; perhaps indeed I went so far as to hope that they would be such as to put all countenance out of the question. I tried to focus the page, in the daily airing, as he perhaps even pushed the bath-chair over somebody's toes. I was destined to hear, however, through Mrs. Saltram (who, I afterward learned, was in correspondence with Lady Coxon's housekeeper) that Gravener was known to have spoken of the habitation I had in my eye as the pleasantest thing at Clockborough. On his part, I was sure, this was the voice not of envy but of experience. The vivid scene was now peopled, and I could see him in the old-time garden with Miss Anvoy, who would be certain, and very justly, to think him good-looking. It would be too much to say that I was troubled by this evocation; but I seem to remember the relief, singular enough, of feeling it suddenly brushed away by an annoyance really much greater; an annoyance the result of its happening to come over me about that time with a rush that I was simply ashamed of Frank Saltram. There were limits after all, and my mark at last had been reached.

I had had my disgusts, if I may allow myself to-day such an expression; but this was a supreme revolt. Certain things cleared up in my mind, certain values stood out. It was all very well to have an unfortunate temperament; there was nothing so unfortunate as to have, for practical purposes, nothing else. I avoided George Gravener at this moment, and reflected that at such a time I should do so most effectually by leaving England. I wanted to forget Frank Saltram—that was all. I didn't want to do any thing in the world to him but that. Indignation had withered on the stalk, and I felt that one could pity him as much as one ought only by never thinking of him again. It wasn't for any thing he had done to me; it was for something he had done to the Mulvilles. Adelaide had cried about it for a week, and her husband, profiting by the example so signally given him of the fatal effect of the want of a character, left the letter unanswered. The letter, an incredible one, addressed by Saltram to Wimbledon, during a stay with the Pudneys at Ramsgate, was the central feature of the incident; which, however, had many features, each more painful than whichever other we compared it with. The Pudneys had

behaved shockingly, but that was no excuse. Base
ingratitude, gross indecency—one had one's choice
only of such formulas as that the more they fitted
the less they gave one rest. These are dead aches
now, and I am under no obligation, thank Heaven,
to be definite about the business. There are things
which, if I had had to tell them—well, I wouldn't
have told my story.

I went abroad for the general election, and if I
don't know how much, on the Continent, I forgot,
I at least know how much I missed him. At a
distance, in a foreign land, ignoring, abjuring,
unlearning him, I discovered what he had done for
me. I owed him, oh, unmistakably ! certain noble
conceptions. I had lighted my little taper at his
smoky lamp, and lo ! it continued to twinkle. But
the light it gave me just showed me how much
more I wanted. I was pursued of course by letters
from Mrs. Saltram, which I didn't scruple not to
read, though I was duly conscious that her embar-
rassments would now be of the gravest. I sacrificed to propriety by simply putting them away,
and this is how, one day as my absence drew to
an end, my eye, as I rummaged in my desk for
another paper, was caught by a name on a leaf
that had detached itself from the packet. The
allusion was to Miss Anvoy, who, it appeared, was
engaged to be married to Mr. George Gravener ;
and the news was two months old. A direct
question of Mrs. Saltram's had thus remained
unanswered—she had enquired of me in a post-

script what sort of man this Mr. Gravener might be. This Mr. Gravener had been triumphantly returned for Clockborough, in the interest of the party that had swept the country, so that I might easily have referred Mrs. Saltram to the journals of the day. But when I at last wrote to her that I was coming home and would discharge my accumulated burden by seeing her, I remarked in regard to her question that she must really put it to Miss Anvoy.

VI

I HAD almost avoided the general election, but some of its consequences, on my return, had smartly to be faced. The season, in London, began to breathe again and to flap its folded wings. Confidence, under the new ministry, was understood to be reviving, and one of the symptoms, in the social body, was a recovery of appetite. People once more fed together, and it happened that, one Saturday night, at somebody's house, I fed with George Gravener. When the ladies left the room I moved up to where he sat and offered him my congratulation. "'On my election?" he asked, after a moment; whereupon I feigned, jocosely, not to have heard of his election and to be alluding to something much more important, the rumor of his engagement. I dare say I colored, however, for his political victory

had momentarily passed out of my mind. What
was present to it was that he was to marry that
beautiful girl ; and yet his question made me conscious of some discomposure—I had not intended
to put that before every thing. He himself indeed
ought gracefully to have done so, and I remember
thinking the whole man was in this assumption
that in expressing my sense of what he had won
I had fixed my thoughts on his "seat." We
straightened the matter out, and he was so much
lighter in hand than I had lately seen him that his
spirits might well have been fed from a double
source. He was so good as to say that he hoped I
should soon make the acquaintance of Miss Anvoy,
who, with her aunt, was presently coming up to
town. Lady Coxon, in the country, had been
seriously unwell, and this had delayed their
arrival. I told him I had heard the marriage
would be a splendid one ; on which, brightened
and humanized by his luck, he laughed and said :
"Do you mean for *her?*" When I had again
explained what I meant he went on : "Oh, she's
an American, but you'd scarcely know it ; unless,
perhaps," he added, "by her being used to more
money than most girls in England, even the
daughters of rich men. That wouldn't in the least
do for a fellow like me, you know, if it wasn't for
the great liberality of her father. He really has
been most kind, and every thing is quite satisfactory." He added that his eldest brother had
taken a tremendous fancy to her, and that during a

recent visit at Coldfield she had nearly won over Lady Maddock. I gathered from something he dropped later that the free-handed gentleman beyond the seas had not made a settlement, but had given a handsome present, and was apparently to be looked to, across the water, for other favors. People are simplified alike by great contentments and great yearnings, and whether or no it was Gravener's directness that begot my own, I seem to recall that in some turn taken by our talk he almost imposed it on me as an act of decorum to ask if Miss Anvoy had also, by chance, expectations from her aunt. My enquiry drew out that Lady Coxon, who was the oddest of women, would have in any contingency to act under her late husband's will, which was odder still; saddling her with a mass of queer obligations complicated with queer loopholes. There were several dreary people—Coxon cousins, old maids—to whom she would have more or less to minister. Gravener laughed, without saying no, when I suggested that the young lady might come in through a loophole; then suddenly, as if he suspected that I had turned a lantern on him, he exclaimed quite dryly: "That's all rot—one is moved by other springs!"

A fortnight later, at Lady Coxon's own house, I understood well enough the springs one was moved by. Gravener had spoken of me there as an old friend, and I received a gracious invitation to dine. The knight's widow was again indisposed—she had succumbed at the eleventh hour; so that I found Miss Anvoy bravely playing hostess, without even Gravener's help, inasmuch as, to make matters worse, he had just sent up word that the House, the insatiable House, with which he supposed he had contracted for easier terms, positively declined to release him. I was struck with the courage, the grace, and gayety of the young lady left to deal unaided with the possibilities of the Regent's Park. I did what I could to help her to keep them down, or up, after I had recovered from the confusion of seeing her slightly disconcerted at perceiving in the guest introduced by her intended the gentleman with whom she had had that talk about Frank Saltram. I had at that moment my first glimpse of the fact that she was a person who could carry a responsibility; but I leave the reader to judge of my sense of the aggravation, for either of us, of such a burden when I heard the servant announce Mrs. Saltram. From what immediately passed between the two ladies I gathered that the latter had been sent for post-haste to fill the gap created by the absence of the mistress of the house. " Good ! " I exclaimed, " she will be put by *me ;* " and my apprehension was promptly justified. Mrs. Saltram taken in to dinner, and taken in as a consequence of an appeal to her amiability, was Mrs. Saltram with a vengeance. I asked myself what Miss Anvoy meant by doing such things, but the only answer I arrived at was that Gravener was verily fortunate. She had not happened to tell him of her visit to Upper Baker

Street, but she would certainly tell him to-morrow; not indeed that this would make him like any better her having had the simplicity to invite such a person as Mrs. Saltram on such an occasion. I reflected that I had never seen a young woman put such ignorance into her cleverness, such freedom into her modesty ; this, I think, was when, after dinner, she said to me frankly, with almost jubilant mirth : "Oh, you don't admire Mrs. Saltram ? "

Why should I ? This was truly an innocent maiden. I had briefly to consider before I could reply that my objection to the lady in question was the objection often formulated in regard to persons met at the social board—I knew all her stories. Then, as Miss Anvoy remained momentarily vague, I added :

"About her husband."

" Oh, yes, but there are some new ones."

" None for me. Oh, novelty would be pleasant! "

" Doesn't it appear that of late he has been particularly horrid ? "

" His fluctuations don't matter," I replied, " for at night all cats are gray. You saw the shade of this one the night we waited for him together. What will you have ? He has no dignity."

Miss Anvoy, who had been introducing with her American distinctness, looked encouragingly round at some of the combinations she had risked. " It's too bad I can't see him."

" You mean Gravener won't let you ? "

"I haven't asked him. He lets me do every thing."

7

" But you know he knows him and wonders what some of us see in him."

" We haven't happened to talk of him," the girl said.

" Get him to take you out some day to see the Mulvilles."

" I thought Mr. Saltram had thrown the Mulvilles over."

" Utterly. But that won't prevent his being planted there again, to bloom like a rose, within a month or two."

Miss Anvoy thought a moment. Then, " I should like to see them," she said, with her fostering smile.

" They're tremendously worth it. You mustn't miss them."

" I'll make George take me," she went on, as Mrs. Saltram came up to interrupt us. The girl smiled at her as kindly as she had smiled at me, and, addressing the question to her, continued : " But the chance of a lecture—one of the wonderful lectures ? Isn't there another course announced ? "

" Another ? There are about thirty ! " I exclaimed, turning away and feeling Mrs. Saltram's little eyes in my back. A few days after this I heard that Gravener's marriage was near at hand —was settled for Whitsuntide : but as I had received no invitation I doubted it, and presently there came to me in fact the report of a postponement. Something was the matter ; what was the matter was supposed to be that Lady Coxon was now critically ill. I had called on her after my dinner in the Regent's Park, but I had neither seen her nor seen Miss Anvoy. I forget to-day the exact order in which, at this period, certain incidents occurred and the particular stage at which it suddenly struck me, making me catch my breath a little, that the progression, the acceleration, was for all the world that of a drama. This was probably rather late in the day, and the exact order doesn't matter. What had already occurred was some accident determining a more patient wait. George Gravener, whom I met again, in fact told me as much, but without signs of perturbation. Lady Coxon had to be constantly attended to, and there were other good reasons as well. Lady Coxon had to be so constantly attended to that, on the occasion of a second attempt in the Regent's Park, I equally failed to obtain a sight of her niece. I judged it discreet under the circumstances not to make a third ; but this didn't matter, for it was through Adelaide Mulville that the side-wind of the comedy, though I was at first unwitting, began to reach me. I went to Wimbledon at times because Saltram was there, and I went at others because he was not. The Pudneys, who had taken him to Birmingham, had already got rid of him, and we had a horrible consciousness of his wandering roofless, in dishonor, about the smoky Midlands, almost as the injured Lear wandered on the storm-lashed heath. His room, up-stairs, had been lately done up (I could hear the crackle of the new chintz), and the difference only made his smirches and bruises, his splendid tainted genius, the more tragic. If he wasn't barefoot in the mire, he was sure to be unconventionally shod. These were the things Adelaide and I, who were old enough friends to stare at each other in silence, talked about when we didn't speak. When we spoke it was only about the brilliant girl George Gravener was to marry, whom he had brought out the other Sunday. I could see that this presentation had been happy, for Mrs. Mulville commemorated it in the only way in which she ever expressed her confidence in a new relation. "She likes me—she likes me": her native humility exulted in that measure of success. We all knew for ourselves how she liked those who liked her, and as regards Ruth Anvoy she was more easily won over than Lady Maddock.

VII

ONE of the consequences, for the Mulvilles, of the sacrifices they made for Frank Saltram was that they had to give up their carriage. Adelaide drove gently into London in a one-horse greenish thing, an early Victorian landau, hired, near at hand, imaginatively, from a broken-down jobmaster whose wife was in consumption—a vehicle that made people turn round all the more when her

pensioner sat beside her in a soft white hat and a
shawl, one of her own. This was his position, and
I dare say his costume, when on an afternoon in
July she went to return Miss Anvoy's visit. The
wheel of fate had now revolved, and amid silences
deep and exhaustive, compunctions and condona-
tions alike unutterable, Saltram was reinstated.
Was it in pride or in penance that Mrs. Mulville
began immediately to drive him about? If he was
ashamed of his ingratitude, she might have been
ashamed of her forgiveness ; but she was incor-
rigibly capable of liking him to be seen strikingly
seated in the landau while she was in shops or with
her acquaintance. However, if he was in the
pillory for twenty minutes in the Regent's Park (I
mean at Lady Coxon's door, while her companion
paid her call) it was, not for the further humiliation
of any one concerned that she presently came out
for him in person, not even to show either of them
what a fool she was that she drew him in to be
introduced to the clever young American. Her
account of the introduction I had in its order, but
before that, very late in the season, under Gravener's auspices, I met Miss Anvoy at tea at the
House of Commons. The member for Clockborough had gathered a group of pretty ladies, and
the Mulvilles were not of the party. On the great
terrace, as I strolled off a little with her, the guest
of honor immediately exclaimed to me ; "I've seen
him, you know—I've seen him ! " She told me
about Saltram's call.

"And how did you find him?"

"Oh, so strange!"

"You didn't like him?"

"I can't tell till I see him again."

"You want to do that?"

She was silent a moment.   "Immensely!"

We stopped; I fancied she had become aware
Gravener was looking at us.   She turned back
toward the knot of the others, and I said: "Dislike him as much as you will—I see you are
bitten."

"Bitten?"   I thought she colored a little.

"Oh, it doesn't matter!" I laughed; "one
doesn't die of it."

"I hope I sha'n't die of any thing before I've
seen more of Mrs. Mulville."   I rejoiced with her
over plain Adelaide, whom she pronounced the
loveliest woman she had met in England; but
before we separated I remarked to her that it was
an act of mere humanity to warn her that, if she
should see more of Frank Saltram (which would be
likely to follow on any increase of acquaintance
with Mrs. Mulville), she might find herself flatten-
ing her nose against the clear, hard pane of an
eternal question—that of the relative importance
of virtue.   She replied that this was surely a subject on which one took every thing for granted;
whereupon I admitted that I had perhaps expressed
myself ill.   What I referred to was what I had
referred to the night we met in Upper Baker
Street—the importance relative (relative to virtue)

of other gifts. She asked me if I called virtue a gift—as if it were handed to us in a parcel on our birthday ; and I declared that this very enquiry showed me the problem had already caught her by the skirt. She would have help, however—help that I myself had once had, in resisting its tendency to make one cross.

" What help do you mean ? "

" That of the member for Clockborough."

She stared, smiled, then exclaimed ; " Why, my idea has been to help *him !* "

She *had* helped him—I had his own word for it that at Clockborough her bedevilment of the voters had really put him in. She would do so doubtless again and again, but I heard the very next month that this fine faculty had undergone a temporary eclipse. News of the catastrophe first came to me from Mrs. Saltram, and it was afterward confirmed at Wimbledon ; poor Miss Anvoy was in trouble—great disasters in America had suddenly summoned her home. Her father, in New York, had had reverses—lost so much money that it was really provoking as showing how much he had had. It was Adelaide who told me that she had gone off alone at less than a week's notice.

" Alone ?   Gravener has permitted that ? "

" What will you have ? The House of Commons ! "

I'm afraid I cursed the House of Commons ; I was so much interested. Of course he would follow her as soon as he was free to make her his

wife ; only she mightn't now be able to bring him
any thing like the marriage-portion of which he
had begun by having the virtual promise. Mrs.
Mulville let me know what was already said ; she
was charming, this American girl, but really these
American fathers ! What was a man to do ? Mr.
Saltram, according to Mrs. Mulville, was of opinion
that a man was never to suffer his relation to
money to become a spiritual relation, but was to
keep it wholesomely mechanical. " *Moi pas com-
prendre!* " I commented on this ; in rejoinder to
which Adelaide, with her beautiful sympathy, explained that she supposed he simply meant that
the thing was to use it, don't you know ? but not
to think too much about it. " To take it, but not
to thank you for it ? " I still more profanely
enquired. For a quarter of an hour afterward she
wouldn't look at me, but this didn't prevent my
asking her what had been the result, that afternoon
in the Regent's Park, of her taking our friend to
see Miss Anvoy.

" Oh, so charming ! " she answered, brightening.
" He said he recognized in her a nature he could
absolutely trust."

" Yes, but I'm speaking of the effect on herself."

Mrs. Mulville was silent an instant. " It was
every thing one could wish."

Something in her tone made me laugh. " Do
you mean she gave him something ? "

" Well, since you ask me ! "

"Right there—on the spot ? "

Again poor Adelaide faltered. "It was to me of course she gave it."

I stared ; somehow I couldn't see the scene. "Do you mean a sum of money ? "

"It was very handsome." Now at last she met my eyes, though I could see it was with an effort. "Thirty pounds."

" Straight out of her pocket ? "

" Out of the drawer of a table at which she had been writing. She just slipped the folded notes into my hand. He wasn't looking ; it was while he was going back to the carriage. Oh," said Adelaide re-assuringly, "I dole it out ! " The dear practical soul thought my agitation, for I confess I was agitated, had reference to the administration of the money. Her disclosure made me for a moment muse violently, and I dare say that during that moment I wondered if any thing else in the world makes people so indelicate as unselfishness. I uttered, I suppose, some vague synthetic cry, for she went on as if she had had a glimpse of my inward amaze at such episodes. "I assure you, my dear friend, he was in one of his happy hours."

But I wasn't thinking of that. " Truly, indeed, these Americans ! " I said. "With her father in the very act, as it were, of swindling her betrothed ! "

Mrs. Mulville stared. "Oh ! I suppose Mr. Anvoy has scarcely failed on purpose. Very likely they won't be able to keep it up, but there it was, and it was a very beautiful impulse."

" You say Saltram was very fine ? "

" Beyond every thing. He surprised even me."

" And I know what *you've* heard." After a moment I added : " Had he peradventure caught a glimpse of the money in the table-drawer ? "

At this my companion honestly flushed. " How can you be so cruel when you know how little he calculates ? "

" Forgive me, I do know it. But you tell me things that act on my nerves. I'm sure he hadn't caught a glimpse of any thing but some splendid idea."

Mrs. Mulville brightly concurred. " And perhaps even of her beautiful, listening face."

" Perhaps even ! And what was it all about? "

" His talk ? It was *à propos* of her engagement, which I had told him about ; the idea of marriage, the philosophy, the poetry, the sublimity of it." It was impossible wholly to restrain one's mirth at this, and some rude ripple that I emitted again caused my companion to admonish me. " It sounds a little stale, but you know his freshness."

" Of illustration ? Indeed I do ! "

" And how he has always been right on that great question."

" On what great question, dear lady, hasn't he been right ? "

" Of what other great men can you equally say

it ? I mean that he has never, but *never*, had a deviation ? " Mrs. Mulville exultantly demanded.

I tried to think of some other great man, but I had to give it up. " Didn't Miss Anvoy express her satisfaction in any less diffident way than by her charming present ? " I was reduced to enquiring instead.

" Oh, yes ! she overflowed to me on the steps while he was getting into the carriage." These words somehow brushed up a picture of Saltram's big shawled back as he hoisted himself into the green landau. " She said she was not disappointed," Adelaide pursued.

I meditated a moment. " Did he wear his shawl ? "

" His shawl ? " She had not even noticed.

" I mean yours."

" He looked very nice, and you know he's really clean. Miss Anvoy used such a remarkable expression—she said his mind is like a crystal ! "

I pricked up my ears. " A crystal ? "

" Suspended in the moral world—swinging and shining and flashing there. She's monstrously clever, you know."

I reflected again. " Monstrously ! "

George Gravener didn't follow her, for late in September, after the House had risen, I met him in a railway-carriage. He was coming up from Scotland, and I had just quitted the abode of a relation who lived near Durham. The current of travel back to London was not yet strong; at any rate, on entering the compartment, I found he had had it for some time to himself. We fared in company, and though he had a blue-book in his lap and the open jaws of his bag threatened me with the white teeth of confused papers, we inevitably, we even at last sociably, conversed. I saw that things were not well with him, but I asked no question until something dropped by himself made, as it had made on another occasion, an absence of curiosity invidious. He mentioned that he was worried about his good old friend Lady Coxon, who, with her niece likely to be detained some time in America, lay seriously ill at Clockborough, much on his mind and on his hands.

"Ah, Miss Anvoy's in America?"

"Her father has got into a horrid hole; lost no end of money."

I hesitated, after expressing due concern, but I presently said: "I hope that raises no objection to your marriage."

"None whatever; moreover, it's my trade to meet objections. But it may create tiresome delays, of which there have been too many, from various causes, already. Lady Coxon got very bad, then she got much better. Then Mr. Anvoy suddenly began to totter, and now he seems quite on his back. I'm afraid he's really in for some big reverse. Lady Coxon is worse again, awfully upset by the news from America, and she sends me word that she *must* have Ruth. How can I give her Ruth? I haven't got Ruth myself!"

"Surely you haven't lost her?" I smiled.

"She's every thing to her wretched father. She writes me every post—telling me to smooth her aunt's pillow. I've other things to smooth; but the old lady, save for her servants, is really alone. She won't receive her Coxon relations, because she's angry at so much of her money going to them. Besides, she's hopelessly mad," said Gravener, very frankly.

I don't remember whether it was this, or what it was, that made me ask if she had not such an appreciation of Mrs. Saltram as might render that active person of some use.

He gave me a cold glance, asking me what had put Mrs. Saltram into my head, and I replied that she was unfortunately never out of it. I happened to remember the wonderful accounts she had given me of the kindness Lady Coxon had shown her. Gravener declared this to be false; Lady Coxon, who didn't care for her, hadn't seen her three times. The only foundation for it was that Miss Anvoy, who used, poor girl, to chuck money about in a manner she must now regret, had for an hour seen in the miserable woman (you could never know what she would see in people) an interesting pretext for the liberality with which her nature overflowed. But even Miss Anvoy was now quite tired of her. Gravener told me more about the crash in New York and the annoyance it had been to him, and we also glanced here and there in other directions ; but by the time we got to Doncaster the principal thing he had communicated was that he was keeping something back. We stopped at that station, and, at the carriage-door, someone made a movement to get in. Gravener uttered a sound of impatience, and I said to myself that but for this I should have had the secret. Then the intruder, for some reason, spared us his company ; we started afresh, and my hope of the secret returned. Gravener remained silent, however, and I pretended to go to sleep ; in fact, in discouragement, I really dozed. When I opened my eyes I found he was looking at me with an injured air. He tossed away with some vivacity the remnant of a cigarette and then he said : " If you're not too sleepy I want to put you a case." I answered that I would make every effort to attend, and I felt it was going to be interesting when he went on : " As I told you a while ago, Lady Coxon, poor dear ! is a maniac." His tone had much behind it—was full of promise. I in-

quired if her ladyship's misfortune were a feature
of her malady or only of her character, and he
replied that it was a product of both. The case
he wanted to put to me was a matter on which it
would interest him to have the impression—the
judgment, he might also say—of another person.
"I mean of the average intelligent man," he said ;
"but you see I take what I can get." There would
be the technical, the strictly legal view ; then
there would be the way the question would strike
a man of the world. He had lighted another
cigarette while he talked, and I saw he was glad
to have it to handle when he brought out at last,
with a laugh slightly artificial, "In fact it's a subject on which Miss Anvoy and I are pulling
different ways."

"And you want me to pronounce between you ?
I pronounce in advance for Miss Anvoy."

"In advance—that's quite right. That's how I
pronounced when I asked her to marry me. But
my story will interest you only so far as your
mind is not made up." Gravener puffed his cigarette a minute and then continued : "Are you
familiar with the idea of the Endowment of
Research ? "

"Of Research ? " I was at sea for a moment.

"I give you Lady Coxon's phrase. She has it
on the brain."

"She wishes to endow——"

"Some earnest and disinterested seeker," Gravener said. "It was a sketchy design of her late

husband's, and he handed it on to her ; setting apart in his will a sum of money of which she was to enjoy the interest for life, but of which, should she eventually see her opportunity,—the matter was left largely to her discretion,—she would best honor his memory by determining the exemplary public use.   This sum of money, no less than thirteen thousand pounds, was to be called the Coxon Fund ; and poor Sir Gregory evidently proposed to himself that the Coxon Fund should cover his name with glory—be universally desired and admired.   He left his wife a full declaration of his views, so far at least as that term may be applied to views vitiated by a vagueness really infantine. A little learning is a dangerous thing, and a good citizen who happens to have been an ass is worse for a community than bad sewerage.   He's worst of all when he's dead, because then he can't be stopped.   However, such as they were, the poor man's aspirations are now in his wife's bosom, or fermenting rather in her foolish brain ; it lies with her to carry them out.   But of course she must first catch her hare."

"Her earnest, disinterested seeker ? "

"The flower that blushes unseen for want of the pecuniary independence necessary to cause the light that is in it to shine upon the human race. The individual, in a word, who, having the rest of the machinery, the spiritual, the intellectual, is most hampered in his search."

"His search for what ? "

"For Moral Truth. That's what Sir Gregory called it."

I burst out laughing. "Delightful, munificent Sir Gregory! It's a charming idea."

"So Miss Anvoy thinks."

"Has she a candidate for the Fund?"

"Not that I know of; and she's perfectly reasonable about it. But Lady Coxon has put the matter before her, and we've naturally had a lot of talk."

"Talk that, as you've so interestingly intimated, has landed you in a disagreement."

"She considers there's something in it," Gravener said.

"And you consider there's nothing?"

"It seems to me a puerility fraught with consequences inevitably grotesque and possibly immoral. To begin with, fancy the idea of constituting an endowment without establishing a tribunal —a bench of competent people, of judges."

"The sole tribunal is Lady Coxon?"

"And any one she chooses to invite."

"But she has invited you."

"I'm not competent—I hate the thing. Besides, she hasn't. The real history of the matter, I take it, is that the inspiration was originally Lady Coxon's own; that she infected him with it; and that the flattering option left her is simply his tribute to her beautiful, her aboriginal enthusiasm. She came to England forty years ago, a thin transcendental Bostonian, and even her odd happy,

8

frumpy Clockborough marriage never really materialized her. She feels indeed that she has become very British—as if that, as a process, as a *Werden*, were conceivable ; but it's precisely what makes her cling to the notion of the ' Fund ' —cling to it as to a link with the ideal."

"How can she cling, if she's dying ? "

" Do you mean how can she act in the matter ? " my companion asked. " That's precisely the question. She can't ! As she has never yet caught her hare, spied out her lucky impostor (how should she, with the life she has led ?), her husband's intention has come very near lapsing. His idea, to do him justice, was that it *should* lapse, if exactly the right person, the perfect mixture of genius and chill penury, should fail to turn up. Ah ! Lady Coxon's very particular—she says there must be no mistake. "

I found all this quite thrilling—I took it in with avidity. " If she dies without doing any thing, what becomes of the money ? " I demanded.

" It goes back to his family, if she hasn't made some other disposition of it."

" She may do that, then—she may divert it ? "

" Her hands are not tied. The proof is that three months ago she offered to make it over to her niece."

" For Miss Anvoy's own use ? "

" For Miss Anvoy's own use—on the occasion of her prospective marriage. She was discouraged— the earnest seeker required so earnest a search.

She was afraid of making a mistake; every one she could think of seemed either not earnest enough or not poor enough. On the receipt of the first bad news about Mr. Anvoy's affairs she proposed to Ruth to make the sacrifice for her. As the situation in New York got worse she repeated her proposal."

"Which Miss Anvoy declined?"

"Except as a formal trust."

"You mean except as committing herself legally to place the money?"

"On the head of the deserving object, the great man frustrated," said Gravener. "She only consents to act in the spirit of Sir Gregory's scheme."

"And you blame her for that?" I asked, with an excited smile.

My tone was not harsh, but he colored a little, and there was a queer light in his eyes. "My dear fellow, if I 'blamed' the young lady I'm engaged to, I shouldn't immediately say so even to so old a friend as you." I saw that some deep discomfort, some restless desire to be sided with, reassuringly, approvingly mirrored, had been at the bottom of his drifting so far, and I was genuinely touched by his confidence. It was inconsistent with his habit; but being troubled about a woman was not, for him, a habit: that itself was an inconsistency. George Gravener could stand straight enough before any other combination of forces. It amused me to think that the combination he had succumbed to had an American

accent, a transcendental aunt, and an insolvent
father ; but all my old loyalty to him mustered to
meet this unexpected hint that I could help him.
I saw that I could from the insincere tone in
which he pursued : "I've criticised her of course,
I've contended with her, and it has been great fun."
It clearly couldn't have been such great fun as to
make it improper for me presently to ask if Miss
Anvoy had nothing at all settled upon herself. To
this he replied that she had only a trifle from her
mother—a mere four hundred a year, which was
exactly why it would be convenient to him that
she shouldn't decline, in the face of this total
change in her prospects, an accession of income
which would distinctly help them to marry.
When I enquired if there were no other way in
which so rich and so affectionate an aunt could
cause the weight of her benevolence to be felt, he
answered that Lady Coxon was affectionate indeed, but was scarcely to be called rich. She could
let her project of the Fund lapse for her niece's
benefit, but she couldn't do any thing else. She
had been accustomed to regard her as tremendously provided for, and she was up to her eyes in
promises to anxious Coxons. She was a woman of
an inordinate conscience, and her conscience was
now a distress to her ; hovering round her bed in
irreconcilable forms of resentful husbands, portion-
less nieces, and undiscoverable philosophers.

We were by this time getting into the whir of
fleeting platforms, the multiplication of lights.

"I think you'll find," I said, with a laugh, "that your predicament will disappear in the very fact that the philosopher *is* undiscoverable."

He began to gather up his papers. "Who can set a limit to the ingenuity of an extravagant woman?"

"Yes, after all, who indeed?" I echoed, as I recalled the extravagance commemorated in Mrs. Mulville's anecdote of Miss Anvoy and the thirty pounds.

IX

THE thing I had been most sensible of in that talk with George Gravener was the way Saltram's name kept out of it. It seemed to me at the time that we were quite pointedly silent about him; but afterward it appeared more probable there had been on my companion's part no conscious avoidance. Later on I was sure of this, and for the best of reasons—the simple reason of my perceiving more completely that, for evil as well as for good, he said nothing to Gravener's imagination. Gravener was not afraid of him; he was too much disgusted with him. No more was I, doubtless, and for very much the same reason. I treated my friend's story as an absolute confidence; but when before Christmas, by Mrs. Saltram, I was informed of Lady Coxon's death without having had news of Miss Anvoy's return, I found myself taking for granted that we should hear no more of these nuptials, in which I now recognized an element incongruous from the first. I began to ask myself how people who suited each other so little could please each other so much. The charm was some material charm, some affinity, exquisite doubtless, yet superficial; some surrender to youth and beauty and passion, to force and grace and fortune, happy accidents and easy contacts. They might dote on each other's persons, but how could they know each other's souls? How could they have the same prejudices; how could they have the same horizon? Such questions, I confess, seemed quenched but not answered, when, one day in February, going out to Wimbledon, I found our young lady in the house. A passion that had brought her back across the wintry ocean was as much of a passion as was necessary. No impulse equally strong, indeed, had drawn George Gravener to America; a circumstance on which, however, I reflected only long enough to remind myself that it was none of my business. Ruth Anvoy was distinctly different, and I felt that the difference was not simply that of her being in mourning. Mrs. Mulville told me soon enough what it was; it was the difference between a handsome girl with large expectations and a handsome girl with only four hundred a year. This explanation, indeed, did not wholly content me, not even when I learned that her mourning had a double cause—learned that poor Mr. Anvoy, giving way altogether, buried under the ruins of his fortune, and leaving next to nothing, had died a few weeks before.

" So she has come out to marry George Gravener ? " I demanded. " Wouldn't it have been prettier of him to have saved her the trouble ? "

" Hasn't the House just met ? " said Adelaide. Then she added : " I gather that her having come is exactly a sign that the marriage is a little shaky. If it were certain, a self-respecting girl like Ruth would have waited for him over there."

I noted that they were already Ruth and Adelaide, but what I said was : " Do you mean that she has returned to make it a certainty ? "

" No, I mean that I figure she has come out for some reason independent of it." Adelaide could only figure as yet, and there was more, as we found, to be revealed. Mrs. Mulville, on hearing of her arrival, had brought the young lady out in the green landau for the Sunday. The Coxons were in possession of the house in Regent's Park, and Miss Anvoy was in dreary lodgings. George Gravener was with her when Adelaide called, but he had assented graciously enough to the little visit at Wimbledon. The carriage, with Mr. Saltram in it but not mentioned, had been sent off on some errand from which it was to return and pick the ladies up. Gravener left them together, and at the end of an hour, on the Saturday afternoon, the party of three drove out to Wimbledon. This was the girl's second glimpse of our great man, and I was interested in asking Mrs. Mulville if the impression made by the first appeared to have been confirmed. On her replying, after consideration, that of course with time and opportunity it couldn't fail to be, but as yet she was disappointed, I was sufficiently struck with her use of this last word to question her further.

" Do you mean that you're disappointed because you judge that Miss Anvoy is ? "

"Yes ; I hoped for a greater effect last evening. We had two or three people, but he scarcely opened his mouth."

" He'll be all the better this evening," I added, after a moment. " What particular importance do you attach to the idea of her being impressed ? "

Adelaide turned her mild, pale eyes on me as if she were amazed at my levity. " Why, the importance of her being as happy as *we* are ! "

I'm afraid that at this my levity increased. " Oh, that's a happiness almost too great to wish a person ! " I saw she had not yet in her mind what I had in mine, and at any rate the visitor's actual bliss was limited to a walk in the garden with Kent Mulville. Later in the afternoon I also took one, and I saw nothing of Miss Anvoy till dinner, at which we were without the company of Saltram, who had caused it to be reported that he was indisposed, lying down. This made us, most of us—for there were other friends present—convey to each other in silence some of the unutterable things which in those years our eyes had inevitably acquired the art of expressing. If an American enquirer had not been there we would have expressed them otherwise, and Adelaide would have pretended not to hear. I had seen her, before the very fact, abstract herself nobly; and I knew that more than once, to keep it from the servants, managing, dissimulating cleverly, she had helped her husband to carry him bodily to his room. Just recently he had been so wise and so deep and so high that I had begun to get nervous —to wonder if by chance there were something behind it, if he were kept straight for instance by the knowledge that the hated Pudneys would have more to tell us, if they chose. He was lying low, but unfortunately it was common wisdom with us that the biggest splashes took place in the quietest pools. We should have had a merry life indeed if all the splashes had sprinkled us as refreshingly as the waters we were even then to feel about our ears. Kent Mulville had been up to his room, but had come back with a face that told as few tales as I had seen it succeed in telling on the evening I waited in the lecture-room with Miss Anvoy. I said to myself that our friend had gone out, but I was glad that the presence of a comparative stranger deprived us of the dreary duty of suggesting to each other, in respect of his errand, edifying possibilities in which we didn't ourselves believe. At ten o'clock he came into the drawing-room with his waistcoat much awry, but his eyes sending out great signals. It was precisely with his entrance

that I ceased to be vividly conscious of him. I
saw that the crystal, as I had called it, had begun
to swing, and I had need of my immediate attention for Miss Anvoy.

Even when I was told afterward that he had, as
we might have said to-day, broken the record, the
manner in which that attention had been rewarded
relieved me of a sense of loss. I had of course a
perfect general consciousness that something great
was going on : it was a little like having been
etherized to hear Herr Joachim play. The old
music was in the air ; I felt the strong pulse of
thought, the sink and swell, the flight, the poise,
the plunge ; but I knew something about one of
the listeners that nobody else knew, and Saltram's
monologue could reach me only through that
medium. To this hour I'm of no use when, as a
witness, I'm appealed to (for they still absurdly
contend about it) as to whether or no on that
historic night he was drunk ; and my position is
slightly ridiculous, for I have never cared to tell
them what it really was I was taken up with.
What I got out of it is the only morsel of the total
experience that is quite my own. The others were
shared, but this is incommunicable. I feel that
now, I'm bound to say, in even thus roughly evok-
ing the occasion, and it takes something from my
pride of clearness. However, I shall perhaps be
as clear as is absolutely necessary if I remark that
she was too much given up to her own intensity of
observation to be sensible of mine. It was plainly

not the question of her marriage that had brought
her back.   I greatly enjoyed this discovery, and
was sure that, had that question alone been involved, she would have remained away.   In this
case, doubtless, Gravener would, in spite of the
House of Commons, have found means to rejoin
her.   It afterward made me uncomfortable for her
that, alone in the lodging Mrs. Mulville had put
before me as dreary, she should have in any degree the air of waiting for her fate ; so that I was
presently relieved at hearing of her having gone to
stay at Coldfield.   If she was in England at all
while the engagement stood, the only proper place
for her was under Lady Maddock's wing.   Now
that she was unfortunate and relatively poor, perhaps her prospective sister-in-law would be wholly
won over.   There would be much to say, if I had
space, about the way her behavior, as I caught
gleams of it, ministered to the image that had
taken birth in my mind, to my private amusement,
as I listened to George Gravener in the railway-
carriage.   I watched her in the light of this queer
possibility—a formidable thing certainly to meet—
and I was aware that it colored, extravagantly
perhaps, my interpretation of her very looks and
tones.   At Wimbledon, for instance, it had seemed
to me that she was literally afraid of Saltram ; in
dread of a coercion that she had begun already to
feel.   I had come up to town with her the next
day and had been convinced that, though deeply
interested, she was immensely on her guard.   She

would show as little as possible before she should
be ready to show every thing.   What this final exhibition might be, on the part of a girl perceptibly
so able to think things out, I found it great sport
to forecast.   It would have been exciting to be
approached by her, appealed to by her for advice ;
but I prayed to Heaven I mightn't find myself in
such a predicament.   If there was really a present
rigor in the situation of which Gravener had
sketched for me the elements, she would have to
get out of her difficulty by herself.   It was not I
who had launched her, and it was not I who could
help her.   I didn't fail to ask myself why, since I
couldn't help her, I should think so much about
her.   It was in part my suspense that was responsible for this ; I waited impatiently to see whether
she wouldn't have told Mrs. Mulville a portion at
least of what I had learned from Gravener.   But
I saw Mrs. Mulville was still reduced to wonder
what she had come out again for, if she hadn't
come as a conciliatory bride.   That she had come
in some other character was the only thing that
fitted all the appearances.   Having, for family
reasons, to spend some time that spring in the west
of England, I was in a manner out of earshot of the
great oceanic rumble (I mean of the continuous hum
of Saltram's thought), and my uneasiness tended to
keep me quiet.   There was something I wanted so
little to have to say that my prudence surmounted
my curiosity.   I only wondered if Ruth Anvoy
talked over the idea of the Coxon Fund with Lady

Maddock, and also somewhat why I didn't hear from Wimbledon. I had a reproachful note about something or other from Mrs. Saltram, but it contained no mention of Lady Coxon's niece, on whom her eyes had been much less fixed since the recent untoward events.

X

ADELAIDE's silence was fully explained later ; it was practically explained when in June, returning to London, I was honored by this admirable woman with an early visit. As soon as she appeared I guessed every thing, and as soon as she told me that darling Ruth had been in her house nearly a month I exclaimed : " What in the name of maidenly modesty is she staying in England for ? "

" Because she loves me so ! " cried Adelaide gayly. But she had not come to see me only to tell me Miss Anvoy loved her ; that was now sufficiently established, and what was much more to the point was that Mr. Gravener had now raised an objection to it. That is, he had protested against her being at Wimbledon, where in the innocence of his heart he had originally brought her himself ; in short he wanted her to put an end to their engagement in the only proper, the only happy manner.

"And why in the world doesn't she do so?" I enquired.

Adelaide hesitated. "She says you know." Then, on my also hesitating, she added : "A condition he makes."

"The Coxon fund?" I cried.

"He has mentioned to her his having told you about it."

"Ah, but so little ! Do you mean she has accepted the trust?"

"In the most splendid spirit—as a duty about which there can be no two opinions." Then said Adelaide after an instant : "Of course she's thinking of Mr. Saltram."

I gave a quick cry at this, which, in its violence, made my visitor turn pale. "How very awful !"

"Awful?"

"Why, to have any thing to do with such an idea one's self."

"I'm sure you needn't !" Mrs. Mulville gave a slight toss of her head.

"He isn't good enough !" I went on ; to which she responded with an ejaculation almost as lively as mine had been. This made me, with genuine, immediate horror, exclaim : "You haven't influenced her, I hope !" and my emphasis brought back the blood with a rush to poor Adelaide's face. She declared, while she blushed (for I had frightened her again), that she had never influenced any body and that the girl had only seen and heard and judged for herself. *He* had influenced her, if I would, as he did every one who had a soul : that word, as we knew, even expressed feebly the power of the things he said to haunt the mind. How could she, Adelaide, help it if Miss Anvoy's mind was haunted ? I demanded with a groan what right a pretty girl engaged to a rising M. P. had to *have* a mind ; but the only explanation my bewildered friend could give me was that she was so clever. She regarded Mr. Saltram naturally as a tremendous force for good. She was intelligent enough to understand him and generous enough to admire.

"She's many things enough, but is she, among them, rich enough ?" I demanded. "Rich enough, I mean, to sacrifice such a lot of good money ?"

"That's for herself to judge. Besides, it's not her own money ; she doesn't in the least consider it so."

"And Gravener does, if not *his* own ; and that's the whole difficulty ?"

"The difficulty that brought her back, yes ; she had absolutely to see her poor aunt's solicitor. It's clear that by Lady Coxon's will she may have the money, but it's still clearer to her conscience that the original condition—definite, intensely implied on her uncle's part—is attached to the use of it. She can only take one view of it. It's for the Endowment, or it's for nothing."

"The Endowment is a conception superficially sublime, but fundamentally ridiculous."

"Are you repeating Mr. Gravener's words?" Adelaide asked.

" Possibly, though I've not seen him for months.
It's simply the way it strikes me too.   It's an old
wife's tale.   Gravener made some reference to the
legal aspect, but such an absurdly loose arrangement has no legal aspect."

"Ruth doesn't insist on that," said Mrs. Mulville ; "and it's for her exactly this technical
weakness that constitutes the force of the moral
obligation."

" Are you repeating her words ?" I enquired.
I forget what else Adelaide said, but she said she
was magnificent.   I thought of George Gravener
confronted with such magnificence as that, and I
asked what could have made two such people ever
suppose they understood each other.   Mrs. Mulville assured me the girl loved him as such a
woman could love, and that she suffered as such a
woman could suffer.   Nevertheless she wanted to
see me.   At this I sprang up with a groan.   " Oh,
I'm so sorry ! when ? "   Small though her sense
of humor, I think Adelaide laughed at my tone.
We discussed the day, the nearest it would be
convenient I should come out ; but before she
went I asked my visitor how long she had been
acquainted with these prodigies.

" For several weeks, but I was pledged to
secrecy."

" And that's why you didn't write ? "

" I couldn't very well tell you she was with me
without telling you that no time had even yet been
fixed for her marriage.   And I couldn't very well

tell you as much as that without telling you what
I knew of the reason of it. It was not till a day
or two ago," Mrs. Mulville went on, "that she
asked me to ask you if you wouldn't come and see
her. Then at last she said that you knew about
the idea of the Endowment."

I considered a little. "Why on earth does she
want to see me?"

"To talk with you, naturally, about Mr. Saltram."

"As a subject for the prize?" This was hugely
obvious, and I presently exclaimed : "I think I'll
sail to-morrow for Australia."

"Well, then—sail!" said Mrs. Mulville, getting
up.

"On Thursday at five, we said?" I frivolously
continued. The appointment was made definite,
and I enquired how, all this time, the unconscious
candidate had carried himself.

"In perfection, really, by the happiest of
chances : he has been a dear. And then, as to
what we revere him for, in the most wonderful
form. His very highest—pure celestial light.
You *won't* do him an ill turn?" Adelaide pleaded
at the door.

"What danger can equal for him the danger
to which he is exposed for himself?" I asked.
"Look out sharp, if he has lately been decorous.
He'll presently take a day off ; treat us to some
exhibition that will make an Endowment a
scandal."

9

"A scandal?" Mrs. Mulville dolorously echoed.
"Is Miss Anvoy prepared for that?"

My visitor for a moment screwed her parasol
into my carpet. "He grows bigger every day."

"So do you!" I laughed, as she went off.

That girl at Wimbledon, on the Thursday afternoon, more than justified my apprehensions. I
recognized fully now the cause of the agitation she
had produced in me from the first—the faint foreknowledge that there was something very stiff I
should have to do for her. I felt more than ever
committed to my fate as, standing before her in the
big drawing-room where they had tactfully left us
to ourselves, I tried with a smile to string together
the pearls of lucidity which, from her chair, she
successively tossed me. Pale and bright, in her
monotonous mourning, she was an image of intelligent purpose, of the passion of duty; but I asked
myself whether any girl had ever had so charming
an instinct as that which permitted her to laugh
out, as if in the joy of her difficulty, into the prig-
gish old room. This remarkable young woman
could be earnest without being solemn, and at
moments when I ought doubtless to have cursed
her obstinacy I found myself watching the unstudied play of her eyebrows or the recurrence of a
singularly intense whiteness produced by the part-
ing of her lips. These aberrations, I hasten to add,
didn't prevent my learning soon enough why she
had wished to see me. Her reason for this was as
distinct as her beauty : it was to make me explain

what I had meant, on the occasion of our first meeting, by Mr. Saltram's want of dignity. It wasn't that she couldn't imagine, but she desired it there from my lips. What she really desired of course was to know whether there was worse about him than what she had found out for herself. She hadn't been a month in the house with him, that way, without discovering that he wasn't a man of monumental bronze. He was like a jelly without a mould, he had to be embanked ; and that was precisely the source of her interest in him and the ground of her project. She put her project boldly before me : there it stood in its preposterous beauty. She was as willing to take the humorous view of it as I could be : the only difference was that for her the humorous view of a thing was not necessarily prohibitive, was not paralyzing.

Moreover she professed that she couldn't discuss with me the primary question—the moral obligation : that was in her own breast. There were things she couldn't go into—injunctions, impressions she had received. They were a part of the closest intimacy of her intercourse with her aunt, they were absolutely clear to her ; and on questions of delicacy, the interpretation of a fidelity, of a promise, one had always in the last resort to make up one's mind for one's self. It was the idea of the application to the particular case, such a splendid one at last, that troubled her, and she admitted that it stirred very deep things. She didn't pretend that such a responsibility was a simple matter ; if it had been, she wouldn't have attempted to saddle me with any portion of it. The Mulvilles were sympathy itself : but were they absolutely candid ? Could they indeed be, in their position—would it even have been to be desired ? Yes, she had sent for me to ask no less than that of me—whether there was any thing dreadful kept back. She made no allusion whatever to George Gravener—I thought her silence the only good taste and her gayety perhaps a part of the very anxiety of that discretion, the effect of a determination that people shouldn't know from herself that her relations with the man she was to marry were strained. All the weight, however, that she left me to throw was a sufficient implication of the weight that he had thrown in vain. Oh, she knew the question of character was immense, and that one couldn't entertain any plan for making merit comfortable without running the gauntlet of that terrible procession of interrogation-points which, like a young ladies' school out for a walk, hooked their uniform noses at the tail of governess Conduct. But were we absolutely to hold that there was never, never, never an exception, never, never, never an occasion for liberal acceptance ; for clever charity, for suspended pedantry—for letting one side, in short, outbalance another ? When Miss Anvoy threw off this enquiry I could have embraced her for so delightfully emphasizing her unlikeness to Mrs. Saltram. " Why not have the courage of one's forgiveness," she asked, "as well as the enthusiasm of one's adhesion?"

"Seeing how wonderfully you have threshed the whole thing out," I evasively replied, "gives me an extraordinary notion of the point your enthusiasm has reached."

She considered this remark an instant with her eyes on mine, and I divined that it struck her I might possibly intend it as a reference to some personal subjection to our fat philosopher, to some aberration of sensibility, some perversion of taste. At least I couldn't interpret otherwise the sudden flush that came into her face. Such a manifestation, as the result of any word of mine, embarrassed me; but while I was thinking how to reassure her the flush passed away in a smile of exquisite good-nature. "Oh, you see, one forgets so wonderfully how one dislikes him!" she said; and if her tone simply extinguished his strange figure with the brush of its compassion, it also rings in my ear to-day as the purest of all our praises. But with what quick response of compassion such a relegation of the man himself made me privately sigh, "Ah, poor Saltram!" She instantly, with this, took the measure of all I didn't believe, and it enabled her to go on: "What can one do when a person has given such a lift to one's interest in life?"

"Yes, what can one do?" If I struck her as a little vague, it was because I was thinking of another person. I indulged in another inarticu-

late murmur—" Poor George Gravener ! " What
had become of the lift *he* had given that interest ?
Later on I made up my mind that she was sore
and stricken at the appearance he presented of
wanting the miserable money. This was the hid-
den reason of her alienation. The probable sincerity, in spite of the illiberality, of his scruples
about the particular use of it under discussion
didn't efface the ugliness of his demand that they
should buy a good house with it. Then, as for
his alienation, he didn't, pardonably enough, grasp
the lift Frank Saltram had given her interest in
life. If a mere spectator could ask that last question, with what rage in his heart the man himself
might ! He was not, like her, I was to see, too
proud to show me why he was disappointed.

XI

I was unable, this time, to stay to dinner; such,
at any rate, was the plea on which I took leave.
I desired in truth to get away from my young
lady, for that obviously helped me not to pretend
to satisfy her. How *could* I satisfy her ? I
asked myself—how could I tell her how much had
been kept back ? I didn't even know, and I certainly didn't desire to know. My own policy had
ever been to learn the least about poor Saltram's
weaknesses—not to learn the most. A great deal

that I had in fact learned had been forced upon me
by his wife. There was something even irritating
in Miss Anvoy's crude conscientiousness, and I
wondered why, after all, she couldn't have let him
alone and been content to entrust George Gravener
with the purchase of the good house. I was sure
he would have driven a bargain, got something
excellent and cheap. I laughed louder even than
she, I temporized, I failed her ; I told her I must
think over her case. I professed a horror of
responsibilities and twitted her with her own
extravagant passion for them. It was not really
that I was afraid of the scandal, of moral dis-
credit for the Fund ; what troubled me most was
a feeling of a different order. Of course, as the
beneficiary of the Fund was to enjoy a simple life
interest, as it was hoped that new beneficiaries
would arise and come up to new standards, it
would not be a trifle that the first of these
worthies should not have been a striking example
of the domestic virtues. The Fund would start
badly, as it were; and the laurel would, in some re-
spects at least, scarcely be greener from the brows
of the original wearer. That idea, however, was
at that hour, as I have hinted, not the source of
anxiety it ought, perhaps, to have been, for I felt
less the irregularity of Saltram's getting the
money than that of this exalted young woman's
giving it up. I wanted her to have it for herself,
and I told her so before I went away. She looked
graver at this than she had looked at all, saying

she hoped such a preference wouldn't make me dishonest.

It made me, to begin with, very restless—made me, instead of going straight to the station, fidget a little about that many-colored Common which gives Wimbledon horizons. There was a worry for me to work off, or rather keep at a distance, for I declined even to admit to myself that I had, in Miss Anvoy's phrase, been saddled with it. What could have been clearer, indeed, than the attitude of recognizing perfectly what a world of trouble the Coxon Fund would in future save us, and of yet liking better to face a continuance of that trouble than see, and in fact contribute to, a deviation from attainable bliss in the life of two other persons in whom I was deeply interested? Suddenly, at the end of twenty minutes, there was projected across this clearness the image of a massive, middle-aged man seated on a bench, under a tree, with sad, far-wandering eyes and plump white hands folded on the head of a stick— a stick I recognized, a stout gold-headed staff that I had given him in throbbing days. I stopped short as he turned his face to me, and it happened that for some reason or other I took in as I had, perhaps, never done before the beauty of his rich, blank gaze. It was charged with experience as the sky is charged with light ; and I felt on the instant as if we had been overspanned and con-joined by the great arch of a bridge or the great dome of a temple. Doubtless I was rendered

peculiarly sensitive to it by something in the way
I had been giving him up and sinking him.
While I met it I stood there smitten, and I felt
myself responding to it with a sort of guilty
grimace. This brought back his attention in a
smile which expressed for me a cheerful, weary
patience ; a bruised, noble gentleness. I had told
Miss Anvoy that he had no dignity, but what did
he seem to me, all unbuttoned and fatigued as he
waited for me to come up, if he didn't seem un-
concerned with small things, didn't seem, in short,
majestic ? There was majesty in his mere uncon-
sciousness of our little conferences and puzzle-
ments over his maintenance and his reward.

After I had sat by him a few minutes I passed
my arm over his big soft shoulder (wherever you
touched him you found equally little firmness) and
said in a tone of which the suppliance fell oddly
on my own ear : "Come back to town with me,
old friend—come back and spend the evening." I
wanted to hold him, I wanted to keep him, and at
Waterloo, an hour later, I telegraphed possessively
to the Mulvilles. When he objected, as regards
staying all night, that he had no things, I asked
him if he hadn't every thing of mine. I had
abstained from ordering dinner, and it was too
late for preliminaries at a club ; so we were reduced to tea and fried fish at my rooms—reduced
also to the transcendent. Something had come up
which made me want him to feel at peace with me,
which was all the dear man himself wanted on

any occasion. I had too often had to press upon
him considerations, irrelevant, but it gives me
pleasure now to think that on that particular
evening I didn't even mention Mrs. Saltram and
the children. Late into the night we smoked and
talked ; old shames and old rigors fell away from
us ; I only let him see that I was conscious of what
I owed him. He was as mild as contrition and as
abundant as faith ; he was never so fine as on a
shy return, and even better at forgiving than at
being forgiven. I dare say it was a smaller matter
than that famous night at Wimbledon, the night
of the problematical sobriety and of Miss Anvoy's
initiation ; but I was as much in it on this occasion
as I had been out of it then. At about 1.30 he
was sublime.

He never, under any circumstances, rose till all
other risings were over, and his breakfasts, at
Wimbledon, had always been the principal reason
mentioned by departing cooks. The coast was
therefore clear for me to receive her when, early
the next morning, to my surprise, it was announced
to me that his wife had called. I hesitated, after
she had come up, about telling her Saltram was
in the house, but she herself settled the question,
kept me reticent, by drawing forth a sealed letter
which, looking at me very hard in the eyes, she
placed, with a pregnant absence of comment, in
my hand. For a single moment there glimmered
before me the fond hope that Mrs. Saltram had
tendered me, as it were, her resignation, and desired

to embody the act in an unsparing form. To bring this about I would have feigned any humiliation ; but after my eyes had caught the superscription I heard myself say with a flatness that betrayed a sense of something very different from relief : " Oh, the Pudneys ! " I knew their envelopes, though they didn't know mine. They always used the kind sold at post-offices with the stamp affixed, and as this letter had not been posted they had wasted a penny on me. I had seen their horrid missives to the Mulvilles, but had not been in direct correspondence with them.

" They enclosed it to me, to be delivered. They doubtless explain to you that they hadn't your address."

I turned the thing over without opening it. " Why in the world should they write to me ? "

" Because they have something to tell you. The worst ! " Mrs. Saltram dryly added.

It was another chapter, I felt, of the history of their lamentable quarrel with her husband ; the episode in which, vindictively, disingenuously as they themselves had behaved, one had to admit that he had put himself more grossly in the wrong than at any moment of his life. He had begun by insulting the matchless Mulvilles for these more specious protectors, and then, according to his wont, at the end of a few months had dug a still deeper ditch for his aberration than the chasm left yawning behind. The chasm at Wimbledon was now blessedly closed ; but the Pudneys, across their persistent gulf, kept up the nastiest fire. I never doubted they had a strong case, and I had been from the first for not defending him—reasoning, if they were not contradicted they would perhaps subside. This was above all what I wanted, and I so far prevailed that I did arrest the correspondence in time to save our little circle an infliction heavier than it perhaps would have borne. I knew, that is, I divined, that their allegations had gone as yet only as far as their courage ; conscious as they were in their own virtue of an exposed place, in which Saltram could have planted a blow. It was a question with them whether a man who had himself so much to cover up would dare his blow ; so that these vessels of rancor were in a manner afraid of each other. I judged that on the day the Pudneys should cease for some reason or other to be afraid they would treat us to some revelation more disconcerting than any of its predecessors. As I held Mrs. Saltram's letter in my hand it was distinctly communicated to me that the day had come—they had ceased to be afraid. "I don't want to know the worst," I presently declared.

"You'll have to open the letter. It also contains an enclosure."

I felt it—it was fat and uncanny. "Wheels within wheels ! " I exclaimed. "There is something for me too to deliver."

"So they tell me—to Miss Anvoy."

I stared ; I felt a certain thrill. "Why don't they send it to her directly ? "

Mrs. Saltram hesitated. "Because she's staying with Mr. and Mrs. Mulville."

"And why should that prevent?"

Again my visitor faltered, and I began to reflect on the grotesque, the unconscious perversity of her action. I was the only person save George Gravener and the Mulvilles who was aware of Sir Gregory Coxon's and of Miss Anvoy's strange bounty. Where could there have been a more signal illustration of the clumsiness of human affairs than her having complacently selected this moment to fly in the face of it? "There's the chance of their seeing her letters. They know Mr. Pudney's hand."

Still I didn't understand; then it flashed upon me. "You mean they might intercept it? How can you imply any thing so base?" I indignantly demanded.

"It's not I; it's Mr. Pudney!" cried Mrs. Saltram, with a flush. "It's his own idea."

"Then why couldn't he send the letter to *you* to be delivered?"

Mrs. Saltram's embarrassment increased; she gave me another hard look. "You must make that out for yourself."

I made it out quickly enough. "It's a denunciation?"

"A real lady doesn't betray her husband!" this virtuous woman exclaimed.

I burst out laughing, and I fear my laugh may have had an effect of impertinence.

"Especially to Miss Anvoy, who's so easily shocked? Why do such things concern *her?*" I asked, much at a loss.

"Because she's there, exposed to all his craft. Mr. and Mrs. Pudney have been watching this; they feel she may be taken in."

"Thank you for all the rest of us! What difference can it make when she has lost her power to contribute?"

Again Mrs. Saltram considered; then very nobly, "There are other things in the world than money," she remarked. This hadn't occurred to her so long as the young lady had any; but she now added, with a glance at my letter, that Mr. and Mrs. Pudney doubtless explained their motives. "It's all in kindness," she continued as she got up.

"Kindness to Miss Anvoy? You took, on the whole, another view of kindness before her reverses."

My companion smiled with some acidity. "Perhaps you're no safer than the Mulvilles!"

I didn't want her to think that, nor that she should report to the Pudneys that they had not been happy in their agent; and I well remember that this was the moment at which I began, with considerable emotion, to promise myself to enjoin upon Miss Anvoy never to open any letter that should come to her in one of those penny envelopes. My emotion and I fear I must add my confusion quickly deepened; I presently should have been as glad to frighten Mrs. Saltram as to think I might by some diplomacy restore the Pudneys to a quieter vigilance.

"It's best you should take *my* view of my safety," I at any rate soon responded. When I saw she didn't know what I meant by this I added : " You may turn out to have done, in bringing me this letter, a thing you will profoundly regret." My tone had a significance which, I could see, did make her uneasy, and there was a moment, after I had made two or three more remarks of studiously bewildering effect, at which her eyes followed so hungrily the little flourish of the letter with which I emphasized them that I instinctively slipped Mr. Pudney's communication into my pocket. She looked, in her embarrassed annoyance, as if she might grab it and send it back to him. I felt, after she had gone, as if I had almost given her my word I wouldn't deliver the enclosure. The passionate movement, at any rate, with which, in solitude, I transferred the whole thing, unopened, from my pocket to a drawer which I double-locked would have amounted for an initiated observer to some such promise.

XII

MRS. SALTRAM left me drawing my breath more quickly and, indeed, almost in pain, as if I had just perilously grazed the loss of something precious. I didn't quite know what it was ; it had a shocking resemblance to my honor. The emotion was the livelier, doubtless, in that my pulses were still shaken with the rejoicing with which, the night before, I had rallied to the rare analyst, the great intellectual adventurer and pathfinder. What had dropped from me like a cumbersome garment, as Saltram appeared before me in the afternoon on the heath, was the disposition to haggle over his value. Hang it, one had to choose! one had to put that value somewhere; so I would put it really high and have done with it. Mrs. Mulville drove in for him at a discreet hour—the earliest she could suppose him to have got up; and I learned that Miss Anvoy would also have come had she not been expecting a visit from Mr. Gravener. I was perfectly mindful that I was under bonds to see this young lady, and also that I had a letter to deliver to her; but I took my time, I waited from day to day. I left Mrs. Saltram to deal, as her apprehensions should prompt, with the Pudneys. I knew at last what I meant—I had ceased to wince at my responsibility. I gave this supreme impression of Saltram time to fade, if it would; but it didn't fade, and, individually, it has not faded even now. During the month that I thus invited myself to stiffen again, Adelaide Mulville, perplexed by my absence, wrote to me to ask why I *was* so stiff. At that season of the year I was usually oftener with them. She also wrote that she feared a real estrangement had set in between Mr. Gravener and her sweet young friend—a state of things only partly satisfactory to her so long as the advantage accruing to Mr. Saltram failed to disengage itself from the merely nebulous state. She intimated that her sweet young friend was, if any thing, a trifle too reserved ; she also intimated that there might now be an opening for another clever young man. There never was the slightest opening, I may here parenthesize, and of course the question can't come up to-day. These are old frustrations now. Ruth Anvoy has not married, I hear, and neither have I. During the month, toward the end, I wrote to George Gravener to ask if, on a special errand, I might come to see him, and his answer was to knock the very next day at my door. I saw he had immediately connected my enquiry with the talk we had had in the railway carriage, and his promptitude showed that the ashes of his eagerness were not yet cold. I told him there was something I thought I ought in candor to let him know ; I recognized the obligation his friendly confidence had laid upon me.

"You mean that Miss Anvoy has talked to you? She has told me so herself," he said.

"It was not to tell you so that I wanted to see you," I replied ; "for it seemed to me that such a communication would rest wholly with herself. If, however, she did speak to you of our conversation, she probably told you I was discouraging."

"Discouraging ?"

"On the subject of a present application of the Coxon Fund."

10

"To the case of Mr. Saltram? My dear fellow, I don't know what you call discouraging!" Gravener exclaimed.

"Well, I thought I was, and I thought she thought I was."

"I believe she did, but such a thing is measured by the effect. She's not discouraged."

"That's her own affair. The reason I asked you to see me was that it appeared to me I ought to tell you frankly that decidedly I can't undertake to produce that effect. In fact I don't want to!"

"It's very good of you, d—— you!" my visitor laughed, red and really grave. Then he said: "You would like to see that fellow publicly glorified—perched on the pedestal of a great complimentary fortune?"

"Taking one form of public recognition with another, it seemed to me, on the whole, I could bear it. When I see the compliments that *are* paid right and left, I ask myself why this one shouldn't take its course. This, therefore, is what you're entitled to have looked to me to mention to you. I have some evidence that perhaps would be really dissuasive, but I propose to invite Miss Anvoy to remain in ignorance of it."

"And to invite me to do the same?"

"Oh, you don't require it; you've evidence enough. I speak of a sealed letter which I've been requested to deliver to her."

"And you don't mean to?"

"There's only one consideration that would make me."

Gravener's clear, handsome eyes plunged into mine a minute, but evidently without fishing up a clew to this motive—a failure by which I was almost wounded. "What does the letter contain?"

"It's sealed, as I tell you, and I don't know what it contains."

"Why is it sent through you?"

"Rather than you?" I hesitated a moment. "The only explanation I can think of is that the person sending it may have imagined your relations with Miss Anvoy to be at an end—may have been told this is the case by Mrs. Saltram."

"My relations with Miss Anvoy are not at an end," poor Gravener stammered.

Again, for an instant, I deliberated. "The offer I propose to make you gives me the right to put a question remarkably direct. Are you still engaged to Miss Anvoy?"

"No, I'm not," he slowly brought out. "But we're perfectly good friends."

"Such good friends that you will again become prospective husband and wife if the obstacle in your path be removed?"

"Removed?" Gravener anxiously repeated.

"If I give Miss Anvoy the letter I speak of, she may drop her project."

"Then, for God's sake give it!"

"I'll do so if you're ready to assure me that her

dropping it would now presumably bring about your marriage."

"I'd marry her the next day!" my visitor cried.

"Yes, but would she marry you? What I ask of you, of course, is nothing less than your word of honor as to your conviction of this. If you give it me," I said, "I'll engage to hand her the letter before night."

Gravener took up his hat; turning it mechanically round, he stood looking a moment hard at its unruffled perfection. Then, very angrily, honestly, and gallantly: "Hand it to the devil!" he broke out; with which he clapped the hat on his head and left me.

"Will you read it or not?" I said to Ruth Anvoy at Wimbledon, when I had told her the story of Mrs. Saltram's visit.

She reflected for a period which was probably of the briefest, but which was long enough to make me nervous. "Have you brought it with you?"

"No, indeed. It's at home locked up."

There was another great silence, and then she said: "Go back and destroy it."

I went back, but I didn't destroy it till after Saltram's death, when I burned it unread. The Pudneys approached her again pressingly, but, prompt as they were, the Coxon Fund had already become an operative benefit and a general amaze: Mr. Saltram, while we gathered about, as it were, to watch the manna descend, was already drawing the magnificent income. He drew it as he had always drawn every thing, with a grand, abstracted gesture. Its magnificence, alas, as all the world now knows, quite quenched him ; it was the beginning of his decline. It was also naturally a new grievance for his wife, who began to believe in him as soon as he was blighted, and who at this hour accuses us of having bribed him, on the whim of a meddlesome American, to renounce his glorious office, to become, as she says, like every body else. The very day he found himself able to publish he wholly ceased to produce. This deprived us, as may easily be imagined, of much of our occupation, and especially deprived the Mulvilles, whose want of self-support I never measured till they lost their great inmate. They have no one to live on now. Adelaide's most frequent reference to their destitution is embodied in the remark that dear far-away Ruth's intentions were doubtless good. She and Kent are even yet looking for another prop, but no one presents a true sphere of usefulness. They complain that people are self-sufficing. With Saltram the fine type of the child of adoption was scattered, the grander, the elder style. They have got their carriage back, but what's an empty carriage ? In short I think we were all happier as well as poorer before ; even including George Gravener, who, by the deaths of his brother and his nephew, has lately become Lord Maddock. His wife, whose fortune clears the property, is criminally dull ; he hates being in the Upper House, and he has not yet had high office. But

what are these accidents, which I should, perhaps, apologize for mentioning, in the light of
the great eventual boon promised the patient
by the rate at which the Coxon Fund must be
rolling up ?

THE MIDDLE YEARS

THE April day was soft and bright, and poor
Dencombe, happy in the conceit of reasserted
strength, stood in the garden of the hotel, com-
paring, with a deliberation in which, however,
there was still something of languor, the attrac-
tions of easy strolls. He liked the feeling of the
south, so far as you could have it in the north, he
liked the sandy cliffs and the clustered pines, he
liked even the colorless sea. "Bournemouth as a
health-resort" had sounded like a mere advertise-
ment, but now he was reconciled to the prosaic.
The sociable country postman, passing through the
garden, had just given him a small parcel, which
he took out with him, leaving the hotel to the
right and creeping to a convenient bench that he
knew of, a safe recess in the cliff. It looked to the
south, to the tinted walls of the Island, and was
protected behind by the sloping shoulder of the
down. He was tired enough when he reached it,
and for a moment he was disappointed ; he was
better, of course, but better, after all, than what ?
He should never again, as at one or two great
moments of the past, be better than himself. The
infinite of life had gone, and what was left of the
dose was a small glass engraved like a ther-

mometer by the apothecary. He sat and stared
at the sea, which appeared all surface and twinkle,
far shallower than the spirit of man. It was the
abyss of human illusion that was the real, the
tideless deep. He held his packet, which had
come by book-post, unopened on his knee, liking,
in the lapse of so many joys (his illness had made
him feel his age), to know that it was there, but
taking for granted there could be no complete
renewal of the pleasure, dear to young experience, of seeing one's self "just out." Dencombe, who had a reputation, had come out too
often and knew too well in advance how he should
look.

His postponement associated itself vaguely, after
a little, with a group of three persons, two ladies
and a young man, whom, beneath him, straggling
and seemingly silent, he could see move slowly
together along the sands. The gentleman had
his head bent over a book, and was occasionally
brought to a stop by the charm of this volume,
which, as Dencombe could perceive even at a distance, had a cover alluringly red. Then his companions, going a little further, waited for him to
come up, poking their parasols into the beach, looking around them at the sea and sky, and clearly
sensible of the beauty of the day. To these things
the young man with the book was still more clearly
indifferent ; lingering, credulous, absorbed, he was
an object of envy to an observer from whose connection with literature all such artlessness had

faded. One of the ladies was large and mature ; the other had the spareness of comparative youth and of a social situation possibly inferior. The large lady carried back Dencombe's imagination to the age of crinoline ; she wore a hat of the shape of a mushroom, decorated with a blue veil, and had the air, in her aggressive amplitude, of cling- ing to a vanished fashion or even a lost cause. Presently her companion produced from under the folds of a mantle a limp, portable chair which she stiffened out and of which the large lady took possession. This act, and something in the move- ment of either party, instantly characterized the performers—they performed for Dencombe's rec- reation—as opulent matron and humble depend- ent. What, moreover, was the use of being an approved novelist if one couldn't establish a rela- tion between such figures ; the clever theory, for instance, that the young man was the son of the opulent matron, and that the humble dependent, the daughter of a clergyman or an officer, nourished a secret passion for him ? Was that not visible from the way she stole behind her protectress to look back at him ? back to where he had let him- self come to a full stop when his mother sat down to rest. His book was a novel ; it had the catch- penny cover, and while the romance of life stood neglected at his side he lost himself in that of the circulating library. He moved mechanically to where the sand was softer, and ended by plumping down in it to finish his chapter at his ease. The humble dependent, discouraged by his remoteness, wandered, with a martyred droop of the head, in another direction, and the exorbitant lady, watching the waves, offered a confused resemblance to a flying-machine that had broken down.

When his drama began to fail Dencombe remembered that he had, after all, another pastime. Though such promptitude on the part of the publisher was rare, he was already able to draw from its wrapper his "latest," perhaps his last. The cover of "The Middle Years" was duly meretricious, the smell of the fresh pages the very odor of sanctity; but for the moment he went no further—he had become conscious of a strange alienation. He had forgotten what his book was about. Had the assault of his old ailment, which he had so fallaciously come to Bournemouth to ward off, interposed utter blankness as to what had preceded it? He had finished the revision of proof before quitting London, but his subsequent fortnight in bed had passed the sponge over color. He couldn't have chanted to himself a single sentence, couldn't have turned with curiosity or confidence to any particular page. His subject had already gone from him, leaving scarcely a superstition behind. He uttered a low moan as he breathed the chill of this dark void, so desperately it seemed to represent the completion of a sinister process. The tears filled his mild eyes; something precious had passed away. This was the pang that had been sharpest during the last few years—the sense of ebbing time, of shrinking opportunity ; and now he felt not so much that his last chance was going as that it was gone indeed. He had done all that he should ever do, and yet he had not done what he wanted. This was the laceration—that practically his career was over ; it was as violent as a rough hand at his throat. He rose from his seat nervously, like a creature hunted by a dread ; then he fell back in his weakness and nervously opened his book. It was a single volume ; he preferred single volumes and aimed at a rare compression. He began to read, and little by little, in this occupation, he was pacified and reassured. Everything came back to him, but came back with a wonder, came back, above all, with a high and magnificent beauty. He read his own prose, he turned his own leaves, and had, as he sat there with the spring sunshine on the page, an emotion peculiar and intense. His career was over, no doubt, but it was over, after all, with *that*.

He had forgotten during his illness the work of the previous year ; but what he had chiefly forgotten was that it was extraordinarily good. He lived once more into his story and was drawn down, as by a siren's hand, to where, in the dim underworld of fiction, the great glazed tank of art, strange, silent subjects float. He recognized his motive and surrendered to his talent. Never, probably, had that talent, such as it was, been so fine. His difficulties were still there, but what was also there, to his perception, though probably, alas ! to nobody's else, was the art that in most cases had surmounted them. In his surprised enjoyment of this ability he had a glimpse of a possible reprieve. Surely its force was not spent—there were life and service in it yet. It had not come to him easily, it had been backward and roundabout. It was the child of time, the nursling of delay; he had struggled and suffered for it, making sacrifices not to be counted, and now that it was really mature was it to cease to yield, to confess itself brutally beaten ? There was an infinite charm for Dencombe in feeling as he had never felt before that diligence *vincit omnia*. The result produced in his little book was somehow a result beyond his conscious intention : it was as if he had planted his genius, had trusted his method, and they had grown up and flowered with this sweetness. If the achievement had been real, however, the process had been manful enough. What he saw so intensely to-day, what he felt as a nail driven in, was that only now, at the very last, had he come into possession. His development had been abnormally slow, almost grotesquely gradual. He had been hindered and retarded by experience, and for long periods had only groped his way. It had taken too much of his life to produce too little of his art. The art had come, but it had come after every thing else. At such a rate a first existence was too short—long enough only to collect material ; so that to fructify, to use the material, one must

have a second age, an extension. This extension
was what poor Dencombe sighed for. As he
turned the last leaves of his volume he murmured :
" Ah, for another go ! ah, for a better chance ! "

The three persons he had observed on the sands
had vanished and then reappeared ; they had now
wandered up a path, an artificial and easy ascent,
which led to the top of the cliff. Dencombe's
bench was half-way down, on a sheltered ledge,
and the large lady, a massive, heterogeneous person, with bold black eyes and kind red cheeks, now
took a few moments to rest. She wore dirty
gauntlets and immense diamond ear-rings ; at
first she looked vulgar, but she contradicted this
announcement in an agreeable off-hand tone.
While her companions stood waiting for her she
spread her skirts on the end of Dencombe's seat.
The young man had gold spectacles, through
which, with his finger still in his red-covered book,
he glanced at the volume, bound in the same
shade of the same color, lying on the lap of the
original occupant of the bench. After an instant
Dencombe understood that he was struck with a
resemblance, had recognized the gilt stamp on the
crimson cloth, was reading "The Middle Years,"
and now perceived that somebody else had kept
pace with him. The stranger was startled, possibly even a little ruffled, to find that he was not the
only person who had been favored with an early
copy. The eyes of the two proprietors met for a
moment, and Dencombe borrowed amusement from

the expression of those of his competitor, those, it might even be inferred, of his admirer. They confessed to some resentment—they seemed to say : " Hang it, has he got it *already* ? Of course he's a brute of a reviewer ! " Dencombe shuffled his copy out of sight while the opulent matron, rising from her repose, broke out : " I feel already the good of this air ! "

" I can't say I do," said the angular lady. " I find myself quite let down."

" I find myself horribly hungry. At what time did you order lunch ? " her protectress pursued.

The young person put the question by. " Dr. Hugh always orders it."

" I ordered nothing to-day—I'm going to make you diet," said their comrade.

" Then I shall go home and sleep. *Qui dort dine !* "

" Can I trust you to Miss Vernham ? " asked Dr. Hugh of his elder companion.

" Don't I trust *you?* " she archly enquired.

" Not too much ! " Miss Vernham, with her eyes on the ground, permitted herself to declare. " You must come with us at least to the house," she went on, while the personage on whom they appeared to be in attendance began to mount higher. She had got a little out of ear-shot ; nevertheless Miss Vernham became, as far as Dencombe was concerned, less distinctly audible to murmur to the young man : " I don't think you realize all you owe the countess ! "

Absently, a moment, Dr. Hugh caused his gold-rimmed spectacles to shine at her.

"Is that the way I strike you?   I see—I see!"

"She's awfully good to us," continued Miss Vernham, compelled by her interlocutor's immovability to stand there in spite of his discussion of private matters.   Of what use would it have been that Dencombe should be sensitive to shades had he not detected in that immovability a strange influence from the quiet old convalescent in the great tweed cape?   Miss Vernham appeared suddenly to become aware of some such connection, for she added in a moment: "If you want to sun yourself here you can come back after you've seen us home."

Dr. Hugh, at this, hesitated, and Dencombe, in spite of a desire to pass for unconscious, risked a covert glance at him.   What his eyes met this time, as it happened, was on the part of the young lady a queer stare, naturally vitreous, which made her aspect remind him of some figure (he couldn't name it) in a play or a novel, some sinister governess or tragic old maid.   She seemed to scrutinize him, to challenge him, to say, from general spite: "What have you got to do with us?"   At the same instant the rich humor of the countess reached them from above: "Come, come, my little lambs, you should follow your old *bergère!*"   Miss Vernham turned away at this, pursuing the ascent, and Dr. Hugh, after another mute appeal to Dencombe and a moment's evident demur, deposited his book on the bench, as if to keep his place or even as a sign that he would return, and bounded without difficulty up the rougher part of the cliff.

Equally innocent and infinite are the pleasures of observation and the resources engendered by the habit of analyzing life. It amused poor Dencombe, as he dawdled in his tepid air-bath, to think that he was waiting for a revelation of something at the back of a fine young mind. He looked hard at the book on the end of the bench, but he wouldn't have touched it for the world. It served his purpose to have a theory which should not be exposed to refutation. He already felt better of his melancholy ; he had, according to his old formula, put his head at the window. A passing countess could draw off the fancy when, like the elder of the ladies who had just retreated, she was as obvious as the giantess of a caravan. It was indeed general views that were terrible ; short ones, contrary to an opinion sometimes expressed, were the refuge, were the remedy. Dr. Hugh couldn't possibly be any thing but a reviewer who had understandings for early copies with publishers or with newspapers. He reappeared in a quarter of an hour, with visible relief at finding Dencombe on the spot, and the gleam of white teeth in an embarrassed but generous smile. He was perceptibly disappointed at the eclipse of the other copy of the book ; it was a pretext the less for speaking to the stranger. But he spoke notwithstanding ; he held up his own copy and broke out pleadingly :

" *Do* say, if you have occasion to speak of it, that it's the best thing he has done yet ! "

Dencombe responded with a laugh : " Done yet " was so amusing to him, made such a grand avenue of the future. Better still, the young man took *him* for a reviewer. He pulled out " The Middle Years " from under his cape, but instinctively concealed any tell-tale look of fatherhood. This was partly because a person was always a fool for calling attention to his work. " Is that what you're going to say yourself ? " he enquired of his visitor.

" I'm not quite sure I shall write any thing. I don't as a regular thing—I enjoy in peace. But it's awfully fine."

Dencombe debated a moment. If his interlocutor had begun to abuse him he would have confessed on the spot to his identity, but there was no harm in drawing him on a little to praise. He drew him on with such success that in a few moments his new acquaintance, seated by his side, was confessing candidly that Dencombe's novels were the only ones he could read a second time. He had come the day before from London, where a friend of his, a journalist, had lent him his copy of the last—the copy sent to the office of the journal and already the subject of a " notice " which, as was pretended there (but one had to allow for " swagger "), it had taken a full quarter of an hour to prepare. He intimated that he was ashamed for

11

his friend, and in the case of a work demanding and repaying study, of such inferior manners ; and, with his fresh appreciation and inexplicable wish to express it, he speedily became for poor Dencombe a remarkable, a delightful apparition. Chance had brought the weary man of letters face to face with the greatest admirer in the new generation whom it was supposable he possessed. The admirer, in truth, was mystifying, so rare a case was it to find a bristling young doctor—he looked like a German physiologist—enamored of literary form. It was an accident, but happier than most accidents, so that Dencombe, exhilarated as well as confounded, spent half an hour in making his visitor talk while he kept himself quiet. He explained his premature possession of " The Middle Years" by an allusion to the friendship of the publisher, who, knowing he was at Bournemouth for his health, had paid him this graceful attention. He admitted that he had been ill, for Dr. Hugh would infallibly have guessed it ; he even went so far as to wonder whether he mightn't look for some hygienic " tip " from a personage combining so bright an enthusiasm with a presumable knowledge of the remedies now in vogue. It would shake his faith a little perhaps to have to take a doctor seriously who could take *him* so seriously, but he enjoyed this gushing modern youth, and he felt with an acute pang that there would still be work to do in a world in which such odd combinations were presented. It was not true, what he had tried for renunciation's sake to believe, that all the combinations were exhausted. They were not, they were not—they were infinite ; the exhaustion was in the miserable artist.

Dr. Hugh was an ardent physiologist, saturated with the spirit of the age—in other words he had just taken his degree ; but he was independent and various, he talked like a man who would have preferred to love literature best. He would fain have made fine phrases, but nature had denied him the trick. Some of the finest in " The Middle Years " had struck him inordinately, and he took the liberty of reading them to Dencombe in support of his plea. He grew vivid, in the balmy air, to his companion, for whose deep refreshment he seemed to have been sent ; and was particularly ingenuous in describing how recently he had become acquainted, and how instantly infatuated, with the only man who had put flesh between the ribs of an art that was starving on superstitions. He had not yet written to him—he was deterred by a sentiment of respect. Dencombe at this moment felicitated himself more than ever on having never answered the photographers. His visitor's attitude promised him a luxury of intercourse, but he surmised that a certain security in it, for Dr. Hugh, would depend not a little on the countess. He learned without delay with what variety of countess they were concerned, as well as the nature of the tie that united the curious trio. The large lady, an Englishwoman by birth and the daughter of a celebrated baritone, whose taste, without his talent, she had inherited, was the widow of a French nobleman and mistress of all that remained of the handsome fortune, the fruit of her father's earnings, that had constituted her dower. Miss Vernham, an odd creature but an accomplished pianist, was attached to her person at a salary. The countess was generous, independent, eccentric; she traveled with her minstrel and her medical man. Ignorant and passionate, she had nevertheless moments in which she was almost irresistible. Dencombe saw her sit for her portrait in Dr. Hugh's free sketch, and felt the picture of his young friend's relation to her frame itself in his mind. This young friend, for a representative of the new psychology, was himself easily hypnotized, and if he became abnormally communicative it was only a sign of his real subjection. Dencombe did accordingly what he wanted with him, even without being known as Dencombe.

Taken ill on a journey in Switzerland the countess had picked him up at an hotel, and the accident of his happening to please her had made her offer him, with her imperious liberality, terms that couldn't fail to dazzle a practitioner without patients and whose resources had been drained dry by his studies. It was not the way he would have elected to spend his time, but it was time that would pass quickly, and meanwhile she was wonderfully kind. She exacted perpetual attention,

but it was impossible not to like her. He gave
details about his queer patient, a " type " if there
ever was one, who had in connection with her
flushed obesity and in addition to the morbid strain
of a violent and aimless will a grave organic dis-
order ; but he came back to his loved novelist,
whom he was so good as to pronounce more essentially a poet than many of those who went in for
verse, with a zeal excited, as all his indiscretion
had been excited, by the happy chance of Dencombe's sympathy and the coincidence of their
occupation. Dencombe had confessed to a slight
personal acquaintance with the author of " The
Middle Years," but had not felt himself as ready
as he could have wished when his companion, who
had never yet encountered a being so privileged,
began to be eager for particulars. He even
thought that Dr. Hugh's eye at that moment
emitted a glimmer of suspicion. But the young
man was too inflamed to be shrewd, and repeatedly
caught up the book to exclaim : " Did you notice
this ? " or " Weren't you immensely struck with
that ? " " There's a beautiful passage toward the
end," he broke out ; and again he laid his hand
upon the volume. As he turned the pages he
came upon something else, while Dencombe saw
him suddenly change color. He had taken up, as
it lay on the bench, Dencombe's copy instead of
his own, and his neighbor immediately guessed the
reason of his start. Dr. Hugh looked grave an
instant ; then he said : " I see you've been altering

the text!" Dencombe was a passionate corrector, a fingerer of style; the last thing he ever arrived at was a form final for himself. His ideal would have been to publish secretly, and then, on the published text, treat himself to the terrified revise, sacrificing always a first edition and beginning for posterity and even for the collectors, poor dears, with a second. This morning, in "The Middle Years," his pencil had pricked a dozen lights. He was amused at the effect of the young man's reproach; for an instant it made him change color. He stammered, at any rate, ambiguously; then, through a blur of ebbing consciousness, saw Dr. Hugh's mystified eyes. He only had time to feel he was about to be ill again—that emotion, excitement, fatigue, the heat of the sun, the solicitation of the air, had combined to play him a trick, before, stretching out a hand to his visitor with a plaintive cry, he lost his senses altogether.

Later he knew that he had fainted and that Dr. Hugh had got him home in a bath-chair, the conductor of which, prowling within hail for custom, had happened to remember seeing him in the garden of the hotel. He had recovered his perception in the transit, and had, in bed, that afternoon, a vague recollection of Dr. Hugh's young face, as they went together, bent over him in a comforting laugh and expressive of something more than a suspicion of his identity. That identity was ineffaceable now, and all the more that he was disappointed, disgusted. He had been rash, been stupid, had gone out too soon, stayed out too long. He oughtn't to have exposed himself to strangers, he ought to have taken his servant. He felt as if he had fallen into a hole too deep to descry any little patch of heaven. He was confused about the time that had elapsed—he pieced the fragments together. He had seen his doctor, the real one, the one who had treated him from the first and who had again been very kind. His servant was in and out on tiptoe, looking very wise after the fact. He said more than once something about the sharp young gentleman. The rest was vagueness, in so far as it wasn't despair. The vagueness, however, justified itself by dreams, dozing anxieties from which he finally emerged to the consciousness of a dark room and a shaded candle.

" You'll be all right again—I know all about you now," said a voice near him that he knew to be young. Then his meeting with Dr. Hugh came back. He was too discouraged to joke about it yet, but he was able to perceive, after a little, that the interest of it was intense for his visitor. "Of course I can't attend you professionally—you've got your own man, with whom I've talked and who's excellent," Dr. Hugh went on. "But you must let me come to see you as a good friend. I've just looked in before going to bed. You're doing beautifully, but it's a good job I was with you on the cliff. I shall come in early to-morrow. I want to do something for you. I want to do every thing.

You've done a tremendous lot for me." The young man held his hand, hanging over him, and poor Dencombe, weakly aware of this living pressure, simply lay there and accepted his devotion. He couldn't do any thing less—he needed help too much.

The idea of the help he needed was very present to him that night, which he spent in a lucid stillness, an intensity of thought that constituted a reaction from his hours of stupor. He was lost, he was lost—he was lost if he couldn't be saved. He was not afraid of suffering, of death ; he was not even in love with life ; but he had had a deep demonstration of desire. It came over him in the long, quiet hours that only with "The Middle Years" had he taken his flight; only on that day, visited by soundless processions, had he recognized his kingdom. He had had a revelation of his range. What he dreaded was the idea that his reputation should stand on the unfinished. It was not with his past but with his future that it should properly be concerned. Illness and age rose before him like spectres with pitiless eyes: how was he to bribe such fates to give him the second chance ? He had had the one chance that all men have—he had had the chance of life. He went to sleep again very late, and when he awoke Dr. Hugh was sitting by his head. There was already, by this time, something beautifully familiar in him.

"Don't think I've turned out your physician," he said ; "I'm acting with his consent. He has

been here and seen you. Somehow he seems to
trust me. I told him how we happened to come
together yesterday, and he recognizes that I've a
peculiar right."

Dencombe looked at him with a calculating
earnestness. "How have you squared the countess ? "

The young man blushed a little, but he laughed.
"Oh, never mind the countess !"

"You told me she was very exacting."

Dr. Hugh was silent a moment. "So she is."

"And Miss Vernham's an *intrigante*."

"How do you know that ? "

"I know every thing. One *has* to, to write
decently ! "

"I think she's mad," said limpid Dr. Hugh.

"Well, don't quarrel with the countess—she's a
present help to you."

"I don't quarrel," Dr. Hugh replied. "But I
don't get on with silly women." Presently he
added : "You seem very much alone."

"That often happens at my age. I've outlived,
I've lost by the way."

Dr. Hugh hesitated ; then surmounting a soft
scruple : "Whom have you lost ? "

"Every one."

"Ah, no ! ". the young man murmured, laying a
hand on his arm.

"I once had a wife—I once had a son. My wife
died when my child was born, and my boy, at
school, was carried off by typhoid."

"I wish I'd been there!" said Dr. Hugh simply.

"Well—if you're here!" Dencombe answered, with a smile that, in spite of dimness, showed how much he liked to be sure of his companion's whereabouts.

"You talk strangely of your age. You're not old."

"Hypocrite—so early!"

"I speak physiologically."

"That's the way I've been speaking for the last five years, and it's exactly what I've been saying to myself. It isn't till we *are* old that we begin to tell ourselves we're not!"

"Yet I know I myself am young," Dr. Hugh declared.

"Not so well as I!" laughed his patient, whose visitor indeed would have established the truth in question by the honesty with which he changed the point of view, remarking that it must be one of the charms of age—at any rate in the case of high distinction—to feel that one has labored and achieved. Dr. Hugh employed the common phrase about earning one's rest, and it made poor Dencombe, for an instant, almost angry. He recovered himself, however, to explain, lucidly enough, that if he, ungraciously, knew nothing of such a balm, it was doubtless because he had wasted inestimable years. He had followed Literature from the first, but he had taken a lifetime to get alongside of her. Only to-day, at last, had he begun to *see*, so that what he had hitherto done was a movement without a direction. He had ripened too late, and was so clumsily constituted that he had had to teach himself by mistakes.

"I prefer your flowers, then, to other people's fruit, and your mistakes to other people's successes," said gallant Dr. Hugh. "It's for your mistakes I admire you."

"You're happy—you don't know," Dencombe answered.

Looking at his watch the young man had got up ; he named the hour of the afternoon at which he would return. Dencombe warned him against committing himself too deeply, and expressed again all his dread of making him neglect the countess—perhaps incur her displeasure.

"I want to be like you—I want to learn by mistakes ! " Dr. Hugh laughed.

"Take care you don't make too grave a one ! But do come back," Dencombe added, with the glimmer of a new idea.

"You should have had more vanity ! " Dr. Hugh spoke as if he knew the exact amount required to make a man of letters normal.

"No, no—I only should have had more time. I want another go."

"Another go ? "

"I want an extension."

"An extension ? " Again Dr. Hugh repeated Dencombe's words, with which he seemed to have been struck.

"Don't you know ?—I want to what they call
' live.' "

The young man, for good-by, had taken his
hand, which closed with a certain force. They
looked at each other hard a moment. "You *will*
live," said Dr. Hugh.

"Don't be superficial. It's too serious ! "

"You *shall* live ! " Dencombe's visitor declared,
turning pale.

"Ah, that's better ! " And as he retired the
invalid, with a troubled laugh, sank gratefully
back.

All that day and all the following night he wondered if it mightn't be arranged. His doctor came
again, his servant was attentive, but it was to
his confident young friend that he found himself
mentally appealing. His collapse on the cliff was
plausibly explained, and his liberation, on a better
basis, promised for the morrow ; meanwhile, however, the intensity of his meditations kept him
tranquil and made him indifferent. The idea that
occupied him was none the less absorbing because
it was a morbid fancy. Here was a clever son of
the age, ingenious and ardent, who happened to
have set him up for connoisseurs to worship.
This servant of his altar had all the new learning
in science and all the old reverence in faith ;
wouldn't he therefore put his knowledge at the
disposal of his sympathy, his craft at the disposal
of his love ? Couldn't he be trusted to invent a
remedy for a poor artist to whose art he had

paid a tribute ? If he couldn't, the alternative was hard : Dencombe would have to surrender to silence, unvindicated and undivined. The rest of the day and all the next he toyed in secret with this sweet futility. Who would work the miracle for him but the young man who could combine such lucidity with such passion ? He thought of the fairy-tales of science, and charmed himself into forgetting that he looked for a magic that was not of this world. Dr. Hugh was an apparition, and that placed him above the law. He came and went while his patient, who sat up, followed him with supplicating eyes. The interest of knowing the great author had made the young man begin "The Middle Years" afresh, and would help him to find a deeper meaning in its pages. Dencombe had told him what he "tried for"; with all his intelligence, on a first perusal, Dr. Hugh had failed to guess it. The baffled celebrity wondered then who in the world *would* guess it; he was amused once more at the fine, full way with which an intention could be missed. Yet he wouldn't rail at the general mind to-day—consoling as that ever had been: the revelation of his own slowness had seemed to make all stupidity sacred.

Dr. Hugh, after a little, was visibly worried, confessing, on enquiry, to a source of embarass-ment at home. "Stick to the countess—don't mind me," Dencombe said repeatedly ; for his companion was frank enough about the large lady's attitude. She was so jealous that she had fallen ill—she resented such a breach of allegiance. She paid so much for his fidelity that she must have it all ; she refused him the right to other sympathies, charged him with scheming to make her die alone, for it was needless to point out how little Miss Vernham was a resource in trouble. When Dr. Hugh mentioned that the countess would already have left Bournemouth if he hadn't kept her in bed, poor Dencombe held his arm tighter and said with decision : "Take her straight away." They had gone out together, walking back to the sheltered nook in which, the other day, they had met. The young man, who had given his companion a personal support, declared with emphasis that his conscience was clear—he could ride two horses at once. Didn't he dream, for his future, of a time when he should have to ride five hundred ? Longing equally for virtue, Dencombe replied that in that golden age no patient would pretend to have contracted with him for his whole attention. On the part of the countess was not such an avidity lawful ? Dr. Hugh denied it, said there was no contract, but only a free understanding, and that a sordid servitude was impossible to a generous spirit ; he liked moreover to talk about art, and that was the subject on which, this time, as they sat together on the sunny bench, he tried most to engage the author of " The Middle Years." Dencombe, soaring again a little on the weak wings of convalescence and still haunted by that happy notion of an

organized rescue, found another strain of eloquence to plead the cause of a certain splendid
"last manner," the very citadel, as it would prove,
of his reputation, the stronghold into which his
real treasure would be gathered. While his
listener gave up the morning and the great still
sea appeared to wait, he had a wonderful explana-
tory hour. Even for himself he was inspired as
he told of what his treasure would consist—the
precious metals he would dig from the mine, the
jewels rare, strings of pearls, he would hang
between the columns of his temple. He was
wonderful for himself, so thick his convictions
crowded ; but he was still more wonderful for
Dr. Hugh, who assured him, none the less, that
the very pages he had just published were already
encrusted with gems. The young man, however,
panted for the combinations to come, and, before
the face of the beautiful day, renewed to Dencombe his guarantee that his profession would
hold itself responsible for such a life. Then he
suddenly clapped his hand upon his watch-pocket
and asked leave to absent himself for half an hour.
Dencombe waited there for his return, but was at
last recalled to the actual by the fall of a shadow
across the ground. The shadow darkened into
that of Miss Vernham, the young lady in attendance on the countess ; whom Dencombe, recognizing her, perceived so clearly to have come to
speak to him that he rose from his bench to
acknowledge the civility. Miss Vernham indeed

proved not particularly civil ; she looked strangely agitated, and her type was now unmistakable.

" Excuse me if I enquire," she said, " whether it's too much to hope that you may be induced to leave Dr. Hugh alone." Then, before Dencombe, greatly disconcerted, could protest : " You ought to be informed that you stand in his light ; that you may do him a terrible injury."

" Do you mean by causing the countess to dispense with his services ? "

" By causing her to disinherit him." Dencombe stared at this, and Miss Vernham pursued, in the gratification of seeing she could produce an impression : " It has depended on himself to come into something very handsome. He has had a magnificent prospect, but I think you've succeeded in spoiling it."

"Not intentionally, I assure you. Is there no hope that the accident may be repaired ?" Dencombe asked.

" She was ready to do any thing for him. She takes great fancies, she lets herself go—it's her way. She has no relations, she's free to dispose of her money, and she's very ill."

" I'm very sorry to hear it," Dencombe stammered.

"Wouldn't it be possible for you to leave Bournemouth ? That's what I've come to ask of you."

Poor Dencombe sank down on his bench. " I'm very ill myself, but I'll try ! "

Miss Vernham still stood there with her colorless

eyes and the brutality of her good conscience.
" Before it's too late, please ! " she said ; and with
this she turned her back, in order, quickly, as if it
had been a business to which she could spare but
a precious moment, to pass out of his sight.

Oh, yes ! after this Dencombe was certainly very
ill. Miss Vernham had upset him with her rough,
fierce news ; it was the sharpest shock to him to discover what was at stake for a penniless young man
of fine parts. He sat trembling on his bench,
staring at the waste of waters, feeling sick with the
directness of the blow. He was indeed too weak,
too unsteady, too alarmed ; but he would make the
effort to get away, for he couldn't accept the guilt
of interference, and his honor was really involved.
He would hobble home, at any rate, and then he
would think what was to be done. He made his
way back to the hotel and, as he went, had a
characteristic vision of Miss Vernham's great
motive. The countess hated women, of course ;
Dencombe was lucid about that ; so the hungry
pianist had no personal hopes and could only console herself with the bold conception of helping
Dr. Hugh in order either to marry him after he
should get his money or to induce him to recognize
her title to compensation and buy her off. If she
had befriended him at a fruitful crisis he would
really, as a man of delicacy, and she knew what to
think of that point, have to reckon with her.

At the hotel Dencombe's servant insisted on his
going back to bed. The invalid had talked about

12

catching a train and had begun with orders to pack ;
after which his humming nerves had yielded to a
sense of sickness. He consented to see his physician, who immediately was sent for, but he wished
it to be understood that his door was irrevocably
closed to Dr. Hugh. He had his plan, which was
so fine that he rejoiced in it after getting back to
bed. Dr. Hugh, suddenly finding himself snubbed
without mercy, would, in natural disgust and to
the joy of Miss Vernham, renew his allegiance to
the countess. When his physician arrived Dencombe learned that he was feverish and that this
was very wrong ; he was to cultivate calmness and
try, if possible, not to think. For the rest of the
day he wooed stupidity ; but there was an ache
that kept him sentient, the probable sacrifice of his
"extension," the limit of his course. His medical
adviser was any thing but pleased ; his successive
relapses were ominous. He charged this personage
to put out a strong hand and take Dr. Hugh off
his mind—it would contribute so much to his being
quiet. The agitating name, in his room, was not
mentioned again, but his security was a smothered
fear, and it was not confirmed by the receipt, at ten
o'clock that evening, of a telegram which his servant
opened and read for him and to which, with an
address in London, the signature of Miss Vernham
was attached. "Beseech you to use all influence
to make our friend join us here in the morning.
Countess much the worse for dreadful journey, but
every thing may still be saved." The two ladies had

gathered themselves up and had been capable in the afternoon of a spiteful revolution. They had started for the capital, and if the elder one, as Miss Vernham had announced, was very ill, she had wished to make it clear that she was proportionately reckless. Poor Dencombe, who was not reckless, and who only desired that every thing should indeed be " saved," sent this missive straight off to the young man's lodging and had on the morrow the pleasure of knowing that he had quitted Bournemouth by an early train.

Two days later he pressed in with a copy of a literary journal in his hand. He had returned because he was anxious and for the pleasure of flourishing the great review of "The Middle Years." Here at least was something adequate—it rose to the occasion ; it was an acclamation, a reparation, a critical attempt to place the author in the niche he had fairly won. Dencombe accepted and submitted ; he made neither objection nor enquiry, for old complications had returned and he had had two atrocious days. He was convinced not only that he should never again leave his bed, so that his young friend might pardonably remain, but that the demand he should make on the patience of beholders would be very moderate indeed. Dr. Hugh had been to town, and he tried to find in his eyes some confession that the countess was pacified and his legacy clinched ; but all he could see there was the light of his juvenile joy in two or three of the phrases of the newspaper. Dencombe couldn't read them, but when his visitor had insisted on repeating them more than once he was able to shake an unintoxicated head. " Ah, no ! but they would have been true of what I *could* have done ! "

" What people ' could have done ' is mainly what they've in fact done," Dr. Hugh contended.

" Mainly, yes ; but I've been an idiot ! " said Dencombe.

Dr. Hugh did remain ; the end was coming fast. Two days later Dencombe observed to him, by way of the feeblest of jokes, that there would now be no question whatever of a second chance. At this the young man stared; then he exclaimed: " Why, it has come to pass—it has come to pass ! The second chance has been the public's—the chance to find the point of view, to pick up the pearl ! "

" Oh, the pearl ! " poor Dencombe uneasily sighed. A smile as cold as a winter sunset flickered on his drawn lips as he added : " The pearl is the unwritten—the pearl is the unalloyed, the *rest*, the lost ! "

From that moment he was less and less present, heedless to all appearance of what went on around him. His disease was definitely mortal, of an action as relentless, after the short arrest that had enabled him to fall in with Dr. Hugh, as a leak in a great ship. Sinking steadily, though this visitor, a man of rare resources, now cordially approved by his physician, showed endless art in guarding him from pain, poor Dencombe kept no reckoning of favor or neglect, betrayed no symptom of regret or speculation. Yet toward the last he gave a sign of having noticed that for two days Dr. Hugh had not been in his room, a sign that consisted of his suddenly opening his eyes to ask of him if he had spent the interval with the countess.

"The countess is dead," said Dr. Hugh. "I knew that in a particular contingency she wouldn't resist. I went to her grave."

Dencombe's eyes opened wider. "She left you ' something handsome ' ? "

The young man gave a laugh almost too light for a chamber of woe. "Never a penny! She roundly cursed me."

"Cursed you ? " Dencombe murmured.

"For giving her up. I gave her up for *you*. I had to choose," his companion explained.

"You chose to let a fortune go ? "

"I chose to accept, whatever they might be, the consequences of my infatuation," smiled Dr. Hugh. Then, as a larger pleasantry : "A fortune be hanged ! It's your own fault if I can't get your things out of my head."

The immediate tribute to his humor was a long, bewildered moan ; after which, for many hours, many days, Dencombe lay motionless and absent. A response so absolute, such a glimpse of a definite result, and such a sense of credit worked together in his mind and producing a strange commotion, slowly altered and transfigured his despair. The

sense of cold submersion left him—he seemed to
float without an effort. The incident was extraordinary as evidence, and it shed an intenser
light. At the last he signed to Dr. Hugh to
listen, and, when he was down on his knees by the
pillow, brought him very near.

"You've made me think it all a delusion."

"Not your glory, my dear friend," stammered
the young man.

"Not my glory—what there is of it! It *is*
glory—to have been tested, to have had our little
quality, and cast our little spell. The thing is to
have made somebody care. You happen to be
crazy, of course, but that doesn't affect the
law."

"You're a great success!" said Dr. Hugh,
putting into his young voice the ring of a marriage bell.

Dencombe lay taking this in ; then he gathered strength to speak once more. "A second
chance—*that's* the delusion. There never was to
be but one. We work in the dark—we do what
we can—we give what we have. Our doubt is
our passion, and our passion is our task. The rest
is the madness of art."

"If you've doubted, if you've despaired, you've
always ' done ' it," his visitor subtly argued.

"We've done something or other," Dencombe
conceded.

"Something or other is every thing. It's the
feasible. It's *you !* "

"Comforter!" poor Dencombe ironically sighed.

"But it's true," insisted his friend.

"It's true. It's frustration that doesn't count."

"Frustration's only life," said Dr. Hugh.

"Yes, it's what passes." Poor Dencombe was barely audible, but he had marked with the words the virtual end of his first and only chance.

THE ALTAR OF THE DEAD.

I

HE had a mortal dislike, poor Stransom, to lean anniversaries, and he disliked them still more when they made a pretence of a figure. Celebrations and suppressions were equally painful to him, and there was only one of the former that found a place in his life. Again and again he had kept in his own fashion the day of the year on which Mary Antrim died. It would be more to the point perhaps to say that the day kept *him :* it kept him at least, effectually, from doing any thing else. It took hold of him year after year with a hand of which time had softened but had never loosened the touch. He waked up to this feast of memory as consciously as he would have waked up to his marriage-morn. Marriage had had, of old, but too little to say to the matter : for the girl who was to have been his bride there had been no bridal embrace. She had died of a malignant fever after the wedding-day had been fixed, and he had lost, before fairly tasting it, an affection that promised to fill his life to the brim.

Of that benediction, however, it would have been false to say this life could really be emptied : it was still ruled by a pale ghost, it was still or-

dered by a sovereign presence. He had not been
a man of numerous passions, and even in all these
years no sense had grown stronger with him than
the sense of being bereft. He had needed no
priest and no altar to make him forever widowed.
He had done many things in the world—he had
done almost all things but one : he had never forgotten. He had tried to put into his existence
whatever else might take up room in it, but he had
never made it any thing but a house of which the
mistress was eternally absent. She was most
absent of all on the recurrent December day that
his tenacity set apart. He had no designed ob-
servance of it, but his nerves made it all their own.
They always drove him forth on a long walk, for
the goal of his pilgrimage was far. She had been
buried in a London suburb, in a place then almost
natural, but which he had seen lose, one after
another every feature of freshness. It was in
truth during the moments he stood there that
his eyes beheld the place least. They looked at
another image, they opened to another light.
Was it a credible future ? Was it an incredible
past ? Whatever it was, it was an immense escape
from the actual.

It is true that, if there were no other dates than
this, there were other memories ; and by the time
George Stransom was fifty-five such memories had
greatly multiplied. There were other ghosts in
his life than the ghost of Mary Antrim. He had
perhaps not had more losses than most men, but

he had counted his losses more; he had not seen
death more closely, but he had, in a manner, felt it
more deeply. He had formed little by little the
habit of numbering his Dead ; it had come to him
tolerably early in life that there was something one
had to do for them. They were there in their simplified, intensified essence, their conscious absence
and expressive patience, as personally there as if
they had only been stricken dumb. When all
sense of them failed, all sound of them ceased, it
was as if their purgatory were really still on earth:
they asked so little that they got, poor things, even
less, and died again, died every day, of the hard
usage of life. They had no organized service, no
reserved place, no honor, no shelter, no safety.
Even ungenerous people provided for the living,
but even those who were called most generous did
nothing for the others. So, on George Stransom's
part, there grew up with the years a determination
that he at least would do something—do it, that is,
for his own—and perform the great charity without
reproach. Every man had his own, and every
man had, to meet this charity, the ample resources
of the soul.

It was doubtless the voice of Mary Antrim that
spoke for them best ; at any rate, as the years
went on, he found himself in regular communion
with these alternative associates, with those whom
indeed he always called in his thoughts the Others.
He spared them the moments, he organized the
charity. How it grew up he probably never could

have told you, but what came to pass was that an altar, such as was, after all, within every body's compass, lighted with perpetual candles and dedicated to these secret rites, reared itself in his spiritual spaces. He had wondered of old, in some embarrassment, whether he had a religion ; being very sure, and not a little content, that he had not at all events the religion some of the people he had known wanted him to have. Gradually this question was straightened out for him ; it became clear to him that the religion instilled by his earliest consciousness had been simply the religion of the Dead. It suited his inclination, it satisfied his spirit, it gave employment to his piety. It answered his love of great offices, of a solemn and splendid ritual ; for no shrine could be more bedecked and no ceremonial more stately than those to which his worship was attached. He had no imagination about these things save that they were accessible to every one who should ever feel the need of them. The poorest could build such temples of the spirit—could make them blaze with candles and smoke with incense, make them flush with pictures and flowers. The cost, in common phrase, of keeping them up fell entirely on the liberal heart.

II

HE had this year, on the eve of his anniversary, as it happened, an emotion not unconnected with that range of feeling. Walking home at the close of a busy day, he was arrested in the London street by the particular effect of a shop-front which lighted the dull brown air with its mercenary grin, and before which several persons were gathered. It was the window of a jeweller whose diamonds and sapphires seemed to laugh, in flashes like high notes of sound, with the mere joy of knowing how much more they were "worth" than most of the dingy pedestrians staring at them from the other side of the pane. Stransom lingered long enough to suspend, in a vision, a string of pearls about the white neck of Mary Antrim, and then was kept an instant longer by the sound of a voice he knew. Next him was a mumbling old woman, and beyond the old woman a gentleman with a lady on his arm. It was from him, from Paul Creston, the voice had proceeded ; he was talking with the lady of some precious object in the window. Stransom had no sooner recognized him than the old woman turned away ; but simultaneously with this increase of opportunity he became aware of a strangeness which stayed him in the very act of

laying his hand on his friend's arm.   It lasted only
a few seconds, but a few seconds were long enough
for the flash of a wild question.   Was *not* Mrs.
Creston dead ?—the ambiguity met him there
in the short drop of her husband's voice, the drop
conjugal, if it ever was, and in the way the two
figures leaned to each other.   Creston, making a
step to look at something else, came nearer, glanced
at him, started, and exclaimed—a circumstance the
effect of which was at first only to leave Stransom
staring—staring back across the months at the different face, the wholly other face the poor man
had shown him last, the blurred, ravaged mask
bent over the open grave by which they had stood
together.   Creston was not in mourning now ; he
detached his arm from his companion's to grasp
the hand of the older friend.   He colored as well
as smiled in the strong light of the shop when
Stransom raised a tentative hat to the lady.
Stransom had just time to see that she was pretty
before he found himself gaping at a fact more
portentous.   " My dear fellow, let me make you
acquainted with my wife."

Creston had blushed and stammered over it, but
in half a minute, at the rate we live in polite
society, it had practically become, for Stransom,
the mere memory of a shock.   They stood there
and laughed and talked ; Stransom had instantly
whisked the shock out of the way, to keep it for
private consumption.   He felt himself grimacing,
he heard himself exaggerating the usual, but he

was conscious that he had turned slightly faint. That new woman, that hired performer, Mrs. Creston ? Mrs. Creston had been more living for him than any woman but one. This lady had a face that shone as publicly as the jeweller's window, and in the happy candor with which she wore her monstrous character there was an effect of gross immodesty. The character of Hugh Creston's wife, thus attributed to her, was monstrous for reasons which Stransom could see that his friend perfectly knew that he knew. The happy pair had just arrived from America, and Stransom had not needed to be told this to divine the nationality of the lady. Somehow it deepened the foolish air that her husband's confused cordiality was unable to conceal. Stransom recalled that he had heard of poor Creston's having, while his bereavement was still fresh, gone to the United States for what people in such predicaments call a little change. He had found the little change ; indeed, he had brought the little change back ; it was the little change that stood there and that, do what he would, he couldn't, while he showed those high front-teeth of his, look like any thing but a conscious ass about. They were going into the shop, Mrs. Creston said, and she begged Mr. Stransom to come with them and help to decide. He thanked her, opening his watch and pleading an engagement for which he was already late, and they parted while she shrieked into the fog, " Mind now you come to see me right away ! " Creston had had the delicacy not to suggest that, and Stransom hoped it hurt him somewhere to hear her scream it to all the echoes.

He felt quite determined, as he walked away, never in his life to go near her. She was perhaps a human being, but Creston oughtn't to have shown her without precautions, oughtn't indeed to have shown her at all. His precautions should have been those of a forger or a murderer, and the people at home would never have mentioned extradition. This was a wife for foreign service or purely external use ; a decent consideration would have spared her the injury of comparisons. Such were the first reflections of George Stransom's amazement ; but as he sat alone that night—these were particular hours that he always passed alone—the harshness dropped from them and left only the pity. *He* could spend an evening with Kate Creston, if the man to whom she had given every thing couldn't. He had known her twenty years, and she was the only woman for whom he might perhaps have been unfaithful. She was all cleverness and sympathy and charm ; her house had been the very easiest in all the world, and her friendship the very firmest. Without accidents he had loved her, without accidents every one had loved her ; she had made the passions about her as regular as the moon makes the tides. She had been also of course far too good for her husband, but he never suspected it, and in nothing had she been more admirable than in the exquisite art with

which she tried to keep every one else (keeping
Creston was no trouble) from finding it out. Here
was a man to whom she had devoted her life and
for whom she had given it up—dying to bring into
the world a child of his bed ; and she had had only
to submit to her fate to have, ere the grass was
green on her grave, no more existence for him
than a domestic servant he had replaced. The
frivolity, the indecency of it made Stransom's eyes
fill ; and he had that evening a rich, almost happy
sense that he alone, in a world without delicacy,
had a right to hold up his head. While he
smoked, after dinner, he had a book in his lap,
but he had no eyes for his page ; his eyes, in the
swarming void of things, seemed to have caught
Kate Creston's, and it was into their sad silences
he looked. It was to him her sentient spirit had
turned, knowing that it was of her he would think.
He thought, for a long time, of how the closed
eyes of dead women could still live—how they
could open again, in a quiet lamplit room, long
after they had looked their last. They had looks
that remained, as great poets had quoted lines.

The newspaper lay by his chair—the thing that
came in the afternoon, and the servants thought
one wanted ; without sense for what was in it, he
had mechanically unfolded and then dropped it.
Before he went to bed he took it up, and this time,
at the top of a paragraph, he was caught by five
words that made him start. He stood staring,
before the fire, at the " Death of Sir Acton Hague,

13

K. C. B.," the man who, ten years earlier, had been the nearest of his friends, and whose deposition from this eminence had practically left it without an occupant. He had seen him after that catastrophe, but he had not seen him for years. Standing there before the fire, he turned cold as he read what had befallen him. Promoted a short time previous to the governorship of the Westward Islands, Acton Hague had died, in the bleak honor of this exile, of an illness consequent on the bite of a poisonous snake. His career was compressed by the newspaper into a dozen lines, the perusal of which excited on George Stransom's part no warmer feeling than one of relief at the absence of any mention of their quarrel, an incident accidentally tainted at the time, thanks to their joint immersion in large affairs, with a horrible publicity. Public, indeed, was the wrong Stransom had, to his own sense, suffered, the insult he had blankly taken from the only man with whom he had ever been intimate ; the friend, almost adored, of his university years, the subject, later, of his passionate loyalty ; so public that he had never spoken of it to a human creature, so public that he had completely overlooked it. It had made the difference for him that friendship too was all over, but it had only made just that one. The shock of interests had been private, intensely so ; but the action taken by Hague had been in the face of men. To-day it all seemed to have occurred merely to the end that George Stransom should think of him

as "Hague," and measure exactly how much he
himself could feel like a stone. He went cold,
suddenly, and horribly cold, to bed.

III

THE next day, in the afternoon, in the great
gray suburb, he felt that his long walk had tired
him. In the dreadful cemetery alone he had been
on his feet an hour. Instinctively, coming back,
they had taken him a devious course, and it was
a desert in which no circling cabman hovered
over possible prey. He paused on a corner and
measured the dreariness; then he became aware
in the gathered dusk that he was in one of those
tracts of London which are less gloomy by night
than by day, because, in the former case, of the
civil gift of light. By day there was nothing, but
by night there were lamps, and George Stransom
was in a mood which made lamps good in themselves. It wasn't that they could show him any
thing; it was only that they could burn clear.
To his surprise, however, after a while, they did
show him something: the arch of a high doorway
approached by a low terrace of steps, in the depth
of which—it formed a dim vestible—the raising of
a curtain, at the moment he passed, gave him a
glimpse of an avenue of gloom with a glow of tapers
at the end. He stopped and looked up, making

out that the place was a church. The thought
quickly came to him that, since he was tired, he
might rest there ; so that, after a moment, he had
in turn pushed up the leathern curtain and gone in.
It was a temple of the old persuasion, and there
had evidently been a function—perhaps a service
for the dead ; the high altar was still a blaze of
candles. This was an exhibition he always liked,
and he dropped into a seat with relief. More than
it had ever yet come home to him it struck him as
good that there should be churches.

This one was almost empty and the other altars
were dim ; a verger shuffled about, an old woman
coughed, but it seemed to Stransom there was
hospitality in the thick, sweet air. Was it only
the savor of the incense, or was it something
larger and more guaranteed ? He had at any rate
quitted the great gray suburb and come nearer to
the warm centre. He presently ceased to feel an
intruder—he gained at last even a sense of community with the only worshipper in his neighborhood, the sombre presence of a woman, in mourning unrelieved, whose back was all he could see of
her, and who had sunk deep into prayer at no great
distance from him. He wished he could sink, like
her, to the very bottom, be as motionless, as rapt
in prostration. After a few moments he shifted
his seat ; it was almost indelicate to be so aware
of her. But Stransom subsequently lost himself
altogether ; he floated away on the sea of light.
If occasions like this had been more frequent in

his life, he would have been more frequently conscious of the great original type, set up in a myriad temples, of the unapproachable shrine he had erected in his mind. That shrine had begun as a reflection of ecclesiastical pomps, but the echo had ended by growing more distinct than the sound. The sound now rang out, the type blazed at him with all its fires and with a mystery of radiance in which endless meanings could glow. The thing became, as he sat there, his appropriate altar, and each starry candle an appropriate vow. He numbered them, he named them, he grouped them—it was the silent roll-call of his Dead. They made together a brightness vast and intense— a brightness in which the mere chapel of his thoughts grew so dim that, as it faded away, he asked himself if he shouldn't find his real comfort in some material act, some outward worship.

This idea took possession of him while, at a distance, the black-robed lady continued prostrate ; he was quietly thrilled with his conception, which at last brought him to his feet in his sudden excitement of a plan. He wandered softly about the church, pausing in the different chapels, which were all, save one, applied to a special devotion. It was in this one, dark and ungarnished, he stood longest—the length of time it took him fully to grasp the conception of gilding it with his bounty. He should snatch it from no other rites and associate it with nothing profane; he would simply take it as it should be given up to him and make

it a masterpiece of splendor and a mountain of fire.
Tended sacredly all the year, with the sanctifying
church around it, it would always be ready for his
offices. There would be difficulties, but from the
first they presented themselves only as difficulties
surmounted. Even for a person so little affiliated
the thing would be a matter of arrangement. He
saw it all in advance, and how bright in especial
the place would become to him in the intermis-
sion of toil and the dusk of afternoons; how rich
in assurance at all times, but especially in the
indifferent world. Before withdrawing he drew
nearer again to the spot where he had first sat
down, and in the movement he met the lady
whom he had seen praying and who was now on
her way to the door. She passed him quickly,
and he had only a glimpse of her pale face and
her unconscious, almost sightless eyes. For that
instant she looked faded and handsome.

This was the origin of the rites more public,
yet certainly esoteric, that he at last found himself
able to establish. It took a long time, it took a
year ; and both the process and the result would
have been—for any who knew—a vivid picture
of his good faith. No one did know, in fact—
no one but the bland ecclesiastic whose acquaintance he had promptly sought, whose objections
he had softly overridden, whose curiosity and
sympathy he had artfully charmed, whose assent to
his eccentric munificence he had eventually won,
and who had asked for concessions in exchange

for indulgences. Stransom had of course at an early stage of his enquiry been referred to the bishop, and the bishop had been delightfully human ; the bishop had been almost amused. Success was within sight, at any rate, from the moment the attitude of those whom it concerned became liberal in response to liberality. The altar and the small chapel that enclosed it, consecrated to an ostensible and customary worship, were to be splendidly maintained; all that Stranson reserved to himself was the number of his lights and the free enjoyment of his intention. When the intention had taken complete effect, the enjoyment became even greater than he had ventured to hope. He liked to think of this effect when he was far from it—he liked to convince himself of it yet again when he was near. He was not often, indeed, so near as that a visit to it had not perforce something of the patience of a pilgrimage ; but the time he gave to his devotion came to seem to him more a contribution to his other interests than a betrayal of them. Even a loaded life might be easier when one had added a new necessity to it.

How much easier was probably never guessed by those who simply knew that there were hours when he disappeared, and for many of whom there was a vulgar reading of what they used to call his plunges. These plunges were into depths quieter than the deep sea-caves ; and the habit, at the end of a year or two, had become the one it would

have cost him most to relinquish. Now they had
really, his Dead, something that was indefeasibly
theirs ; and he liked to think that they might, in
cases, be the Dead of others, as well as that the
Dead of others might be invoked there under the
protection of what he had done. Whoever bent
a knee on the carpet he had laid down appeared
to him to act in the spirit of his intention. Each
of his lights had a name for him, and from time
to time a new light was kindled. This was what
he had fundamentally agreed for, that there
should always be room for them all. What those
who passed or lingered saw was simply the most
resplendent of the altars, called suddenly into
vivid usefulness, with a quiet elderly man, for
whom it evidently had a fascination, often seated
there in a maze or a doze ; but half the satisfaction of the spot, for this mysterious and fitful worshipper, was that he found the years of his life
there, and the ties, the affections, the struggles,
the submissions, the conquests, if there had been
such a record of that adventurous journey in
which the beginnings and the endings of human
relations are the lettered mile-stones. He had in
general little taste for the past as a past of his
own history; at other times and in other places,
it mostly seemed to him pitiful to consider and
impossible to repair; but on these occasions he accepted it with something of that positive gladness
with which one adjusts one's self to an ache that
is beginning to succumb to treatment. To the

treatment of time the malady of life begins at a given moment to succumb ; and these were doubtless the hours at which that truth most came home to him. The day was written for him there on which he had first become acquainted with death, and the successive phases of the acquaintance were each marked with a flame.

The flames were gathering thick at present, for Stransom had entered that dark defile of our earthly descent in which some one dies every day. It was only yesterday that Kate Creston had flashed out her white fire; yet already there were younger stars ablaze on the tips of the tapers. Various persons in whom his interest had not been intense drew closer to him by entering this company. He went over it, head by head, till he felt like the shepherd of a huddled flock, with all a shepherd's vision of differences imperceptible. He knew his candles apart, up to the color of the flame, and would still have known them had their positions all been changed. To other imaginations they might stand for other things—that they should stand for something to be hushed before was all he desired ; but he was intensely conscious of the personal note of each and of the distinguishable way it contributed to the concert. There were hours at which he almost caught himself wishing that certain of his friends would now die, that he might establish with them in this manner a connection more charming than, as it happened, it was possible to enjoy with them in

life. In regard to those from whom one was separated by the long curves of the globe such a connection could only be an improvement; it brought
them instantly within reach. Of course there were
gaps in the constellation, for Stransom knew he
could only pretend to act for his own, and it was
not every figure passing before his eyes into the
great obscure that was entitled to a memorial.
There was a strange sanctification in death, but
some characters were more sanctified by being forgotten than by being remembered. The greatest
blank in the shining page was the memory of
Acton Hague, of which he inveterately tried to
rid himself. For Acton Hague no flame could
ever rise on any altar of his.

IV

EVERY year, the day he walked back from the
great graveyard, he went to church as he had
done the day his idea was born. It was on this
occasion, as it happened, after a year had passed,
that he began to observe his altar to be haunted
by a worshipper at least as frequent as himself.
Others of the faithful, and in the rest of the
church, came and went, appealing sometimes,
when they disappeared, to a vague or to a particular recognition; but this unfailing presence was
always to be observed when he arrived and still

in possession when he departed. He was surprised, the first time, at the promptitude with which it assumed an identity for him—the identity of the lady whom, two years before, on his anniversary, he had seen so intensely bowed, and of whose tragic face he had had so flitting a vision. Given the time that had elapsed, his recollection of her was fresh enough to make him wonder. Of himself she had, of course, no impression, or, rather, she had none at first. The time came when her manner of transacting her business suggested to him that she had gradually guessed his call to be of the same order. She used his altar for her own purpose ; he could only hope that, sad and solitary as she always struck him, she used it for her own Dead. There were interruptions, infidelities, all on his part, calls to other associations and duties ; but as the months went on he found her whenever he returned, and he ended by taking pleasure in the thought that he had given her almost the contentment he had given himself. They worshipped side by side so often that there were moments when he wished he might be sure, so straight did their prospect stretch away of growing old together in their rites. She was younger than he, but she looked as if her Dead were at least as numerous as his candles. She had no color, no sound, no fault, and another of the things about which he had made up his mind was that she had no fortune. She was always black-robed, as if she had had a succession of sorrows. People were not poor, after all, whom so many losses could overtake; they were positively rich when they had so much to give up. But the air of this devoted and indifferent woman, who always made, in any attitude, a beautiful, accidental line, conveyed somehow to Stransom that she had known more kinds of trouble than one.

He had a great love of music and little time for the joy of it; but occasionally, when workaday noises were muffled by Saturday afternoons, it used to come back to him that there were glories. There were, moreover, friends who reminded him of this, and side by side with whom he found himself sitting out concerts. On one of these winter evenings, in St. James' Hall, he became aware, after he had seated himself, that the lady he had so often seen at church was in the place next him and was evidently alone, as he also this time happened to be. She was at first too absorbed in the consideration of the programme to heed him, but when she at last glanced at him he took advantage of the movement to speak to her, greeting her with the remark that he felt as if he already knew her. She smiled as she said : "Oh, yes! I recognize you." Yet in spite of this admission of their long acquaintance it was the first time he had ever seen her smile. The effect of it was suddenly to contribute more to that acquaintance than all the previous meetings had done. He hadn't "taken in," he said to himself, that she was so pretty.

Later that evening (it was while he rolled along in a hansom on his way to dine out) he added that he hadn't taken in that she was so interesting. The next morning, in the midst of his work, he quite suddenly and irrelevantly reflected that his impression of her, beginning so far back, was like a winding river that had at last reached the sea.

His work was indeed blurred a little, all that day, by the sense of what had now passed between them. It wasn't much, but it had just made the difference. They had listened together to Beethoven and Schumann ; they had talked in the pauses and at the end, when at the door, to which they moved together, he had asked her if he could help her in the matter of getting away. She had thanked him and put up her umbrella, slipping into the crowd without an allusion to their meeting yet again, and leaving him to remember at leisure that not a word had been exchanged about the place in which they frequently met. This circumstance seemed to him at one moment natural enough and at another perverse. She mightn't in the least have recognized his warrant for speaking to her ; and yet, if she hadn't, he would have judged her an underbred woman. It was odd that, when nothing had really ever brought them together, he should have been able successfully to assume that they were in a manner old friends— that this negative quantity was somehow more than they could express. His success, it was true,

had been qualified by her quick escape, so that
there grew up in him an absurd desire to put it to
some better test. Save in so far as some other
improbable accident might assist him, such a test
could be only to meet her afresh at church. Left
to himself he would have gone to church the very
next afternoon, just for the curiosity of seeing if
he should find her there. But he was not left to
himself, a fact he discovered quite at the last, after
he had virtually made up his mind to go. The
influence that kept him away really revealed to
him how little to himself his Dead ever left him.
They reminded him that he went only for them—
for nothing else in the world.

The force of this reminder kept him away ten
days ; he hated to connect the place with any
thing but his offices, or to give a glimpse of the
curiosity that had been on the point of moving
him. It was absurd to weave a tangle about a
matter so simple as a custom of devotion that
might so easily have been daily or hourly ; yet the
tangle got itself woven. He was sorry, he was
disappointed ; it was as if a long, happy spell had
been broken and he had lost a familiar security.
At the last, however, he asked himself if he was
to stay away forever from the fear of this muddle
about motives. After an interval, neither longer
nor shorter than usual, he re-entered the church
with a clear conviction that he should scarcely
heed the presence or the absence of the lady of
the concert. This indifference didn't prevent his

instantly perceiving that for the only time since he had first seen her she was not on the spot. He had now no scruple about giving her time to arrive, but she didn't arrive, and when he went away still missing her he was quite profanely and consentingly sorry. If her absence made the tangle more intricate, that was only her fault. By the end of another year it was very intricate indeed ; but by that time he didn't in the least care, and it was only his cultivated consciousness that had given him scruples. Three times in three months he had gone to church without finding her, and he felt that he had not needed these occasions to show him that his suspense had quite dropped. Yet it was, incongruously, not indifference, but a refinement of delicacy that had kept him from asking the sacristan, who would of course immediately have recognized his description of her, whether she had been seen at other hours. His delicacy had kept him from asking any question about her at any time, and it was exactly the same virtue that had left him so free to be decently civil to her at the concert.

This happy advantage now served him anew, enabling him when she finally met his eyes—it was after a fourth trial—to determine without hesitation to wait till she should retire. He joined her in the street as soon as she had done so, and asked her if he might accompany her a certain distance. With her placid permission he went as far as a house in the neighborhood at which she had business ; she let him know it was not where she lived. She lived, as she said, in a mere slum, with an old aunt, a person in connection with whom she spoke of the engrossment of humdrum duties and regular occupations. She was not, the mourning niece, in her first youth, and her vanished freshness had left something behind which, for Stransom, represented the proof that it had been tragically sacrificed. Whatever she gave him the assurance of she gave it without references. She might in fact have been a divorced duchess, and she might have been an old maid who taught the harp.

V

They fell at last into the way of walking together almost every time they met, though, for a long time, they never met anywhere save at church. He couldn't ask her to come and see him, and, as if she had not a proper place to receive him, she never invited him. As much as himself she knew the world of London, but from an undiscussed instinct of privacy they haunted the region not mapped on the social chart. On the return she always made him leave her at the same corner. She looked with him, as a pretext for a pause, at the depressed things in suburban shopfronts ; and there was never a word he had

said to her that she had not beautifully understood. For long ages he never knew her name,
any more than she had ever pronounced his own ;
but it was not their names that mattered, it was
only their perfect practice and their common
need.

These things made their whole relation so impersonal that they had not the rules or reasons
people found in ordinary friendships. They
didn't care for the things it was supposed necessary to care for in the intercourse of the world.
They ended one day (they never knew which of
them expressed it first) by throwing out the idea
that they didn't care for each other. Over this
idea they grew quite intimate ; they rallied to it
in a way that marked a fresh start in their confidence. If to feel deeply together about certain
things wholly distinct from themselves didn't con-
stitute a safety, where was safety to be looked
for ? Not lightly nor often, not without occasion
nor without emotion, any more than in any other
reference by serious people to a mystery of their
faith ; but when something had happened to
warm, as it were, the air for it, they came as near
as they could come to calling their Dead by name.
They felt it was coming very near to utter their
thought at all. The word "they" expressed
enough ; it limited the mention, it had a dignity
of its own, and if, in their talk, you had heard our
friends use it, you might have taken them for a
pair of pagans of old alluding decently to the

14

domesticated gods. They never knew—at least
Stransom never knew—how they had learned to be
sure about each other. If it had been with each a
question of what the other was there for, the certi-
tude had come in some fine way of its own. Any
faith, after all, has the instinct of propagation, and
it was as natural as it was beautiful that they
should have taken pleasure on the spot in the
imagination of a following. If the following was
for each but a following of one, it had proved in
the event to be sufficient. Her debt, however, of
course, was much greater than his, because while
she had only given him a worshipper he had given
her a magnificent temple. Once she said she
pitied him for the length of his list (she had
counted his candles almost as often as himself)
and this made him wonder what could have been
the length of hers. He had wondered before at
the coincidence of their losses, especially as from
time to time a new candle was set up. On some
occasion some accident led him to express this
curiosity, and she answered as if she was surprised
that he hadn't already understood. "Oh, for me,
you know, the more there are the better—there
could never be too many. I should like hundreds
and hundreds—I should like thousands ; I should
like a perfect mountain of light."

Then, of course, in a flash, he understood.
" Your Dead are only One ? "

She hesitated as she had never hesitated. "Only
One," she answered, coloring as if now he knew

her innermost secret. It really made him feel that he knew less than before, so difficult was it for him to reconstitute a life in which a single experience had reduced all others to nought. His own life, round its central hollow, had been packed close enough. After this she appeared to have regretted her confession, though at the moment she spoke there had been pride in her very embarrassment. She declared to him that his own was the larger, the dearer possession—the portion one would have chosen if one had been able to choose ; she assured him she could perfectly imagine some of the echoes with which his silences were peopled. He knew she couldn't ; one's relation to what one had loved and hated had been a relation too distinct from the relations of others. But this didn't affect the fact that they were growing old together in their piety. She was a feature of that piety, but even at the ripe stage of acquaintance in which they occasionally arranged to meet at a concert, or to go together to an exhibition, she was not a feature of any thing else. The most that happened was that his worship became paramount. Friend by friend dropped away till at last there were more emblems on his altar than houses left him to enter. She was more than any other the friend who remained, but she was unknown to all the rest. Once when she had discovered, as they called it, a new star, she used the expression that the chapel at last was full.

"Oh, no!" Stransom replied, "there is a great thing wanting for that! The chapel will never be full till a candle is set up before which all the others will pale. It will be the tallest candle of all."

Her mild wonder rested on him. "What candle do you mean?"

"I mean, dear lady, my own."

He had learned after a long time that she earned money by her pen, writing under a designation that she never told him in magazines that he never saw. She knew too well what he couldn't read and what she couldn't write, and she taught him to cultivate indifference with a success that did much for their good relations. Her invisible industry was a convenience to him; it helped his contented thought of her, the thought that rested in the dignity of her proud, obscure life, her little remunerated art and her little impenetrable home. Lost, with her obscure relative, in her dim suburban world, she came to the surface for him in distant places. She was really the priestess of his altar, and whenever he quitted England he committed it to her keeping. She proved to him afresh that women have more of the spirit of religion than men; he felt his fidelity pale and faint in comparison with hers. He often said to her that since he had so little time to live he rejoiced in her having so much; so glad was he to think she would guard the temple when he should have ceased. He had a great plan for that, which, of course, he told her, too, a bequest of money to keep it up in undiminished state. Of the administration of this fund he would appoint her superintendent, and, if the spirit should move her, she might kindle a taper even for him.

"And who will kindle one even for me ?" she gravely enquired.

VI

SHE was always in mourning, yet the day he came back from the longest absence he had yet made her appearance immediately told him she had lately had a bereavement. They met on this occasion as she was leaving the church, so that, postponing his own entrance, he instantly offered to turn round and walk away with her. She considered, then she said : " Go in now, but come and see me in an hour." He knew the small vista of her street, closed at the end and as dreary as an empty pocket, where the pairs of shabby little houses, semi-detached but indissolubly united, were like married couples on bad terms. Often, however, as he had gone to the beginning, he had never gone beyond. Her aunt was dead—that he immediately guessed, as well as that it made a difference ; but when she had for the first time mentioned her number he found himself, on her leaving him, not a little agitated by this sudden

liberality. She was not a person with whom, after
all, one got on so very fast ; it had taken him
months and months to learn her name, years and
years to learn her address. If she had looked, on
this reunion, so much older to him, how in the
world did he look to her ? She had reached the
period of life that he had long since reached, when,
after separations, the dreadful clock-face of the
friend we meet announces the hour we have tried
to forget. He couldn't have said what he expected, as, at the end of his waiting, he turned the
corner at which, for years, he had always paused ;
simply not to pause was a sufficient cause for
emotion. It was an event, somehow ; and in all
their long acquaintance there had never been such
a thing. The event grew larger when, five minutes
later, in the faint elegance of her little drawing-
room, she quavered out some greeting which
showed the measure she took of it. He had a
strange sense of having come for something in
particular ; strange because, literally, there was
nothing particular between them, nothing save that
they were at one on their great point, which had
long ago become a magnificent matter of course.
It was true that, after she had said, " You can
always come now, you know," the thing he was
there for seemed already to have happened. He
asked her if it was the death of her aunt that made
the difference ; to which she replied : " She never
knew I knew you. I wished her not to." The
beautiful clearness of her candor—her faded beauty

was like a summer twilight—disconnected the
words from any image of deceit. They might
have struck him as the record of a deep dissimula-
tion ; but she had always given him a sense of
noble reasons. The vanished aunt was present, as
he looked about him, in the small complacencies of
the room, the beaded velvet and the fluted moreen ;
and though, as we know, he had the worship of the
dead, he found himself not definitely regretting
this lady. If she was not in his long list, however, she was in her niece's short one, and Stransom presently observed to his friend that now, at
least, in the place they haunted together, she would
have another object of devotion.

" Yes, I shall have another. She was very kind
to me. It's that that makes the difference."

He judged, wondering a good deal before he
made any motion to leave her, that the difference
would somehow be very great and would consist of
still other things than her having let him come in.
It rather chilled him, for they had been happy
together as they were. He extracted from her at
any rate an intimation that she should now have
larger means, that her aunt's tiny fortune had come
to her, so that there was henceforth only one to
consume what had formerly been made to suffice
for two. This was a joy to Stransom, because it
had hitherto been equally impossible for him either
to offer her presents or to find contentment in not
doing so. It was too ugly to be at her side that
way, abounding himself and yet not able to over-

flow—a demonstration that would have been a
signally false note. Even her better situation too
seemed only to draw out in a sense the loneliness
of her future. It would merely help her to live
more and more for their small ceremonial, at a
time when he himself had begun wearily to feel
that, having set it in motion, he might depart.
When they had sat a while in the pale parlor she
got up and said : " This isn't *my* room : let us go
into mine." They had only to cross the narrow
hall, as he found, to pass into quite another air.
When she had closed the door of the second room,
as she called it, he felt that he had at last real
possession of her. The place had the flush of life
—it was expressive ; its dark red walls were articu-
late with memories and relics. These were simple
things—photographs and water-colors, scraps of
writing framed and ghosts of flowers embalmed ;
but only a moment was needed to show him they
had a common meaning. It was here that she had
lived and worked ; and she had already told him
she would make no change of scene. He saw that
the objects about her mainly had reference to certain places and times ; but after a minute he distinguished among them a small portrait of a gentleman. At a distance and without their glasses his
eyes were only caught by it enough to feel a vague
curiosity. Presently this impulse carried him
nearer, and in another moment he was staring at
the picture in stupefaction and with the sense that
some sound had broken from him. He was further

conscious that he showed his companion a white face when he turned round on her with the exclamation : " Acton Hague ! "

She gave him back his astonishment. " Did you know him? "

" He was the friend of all my youth—my early manhood. And *you* knew him? "

She colored at this, and for a moment her answer failed ; her eyes took in every thing in the place, and a strange irony reached her lips as she echoed : " Knew him ? "

Then Stransom understood, while the room heaved like the cabin of a ship, that its whole contents cried out with him, that it was a museum in his honor, that all her later years had been addressed to him, and that the shrine he himself had reared had been passionately converted to this use. It was all for Acton Hague that she had kneeled every day at his altar. What need had there been for a consecrated candle when he was present in the whole array ? The revelation seemed to smite our friend in the face, and he dropped into a seat and sat silent. He had quickly become aware that she was shocked at the vision of his own shock, but as she sank on the sofa beside him and laid her hand on his arm he perceived almost as soon that she was unable to resent it as much as she would have liked.

VII

He learned in that instant two things : one of them was that even in so long a time she had gathered no knowledge of his great intimacy and his great quarrel ; the other was that, in spite of this ignorance, strangely enough, she supplied on the spot a reason for his confusion. " How extraordinary," he presently exclaimed, " that we should never have known ! "

She gave a wan smile, which seemed to Stransom stranger even than the fact itself. " I never, never spoke of him."

Stransom looked about the room again. " Why then, if your life had been so full of him ? "

" Mayn't I put you that question as well. Hadn't your life also been full of him ? "

" Any one's, every one's life was who had the wonderful experience of knowing him. I never spoke of him," Stransom added in a moment, " because he did me—years ago—an unforgetable wrong." She was silent, and with the full effect of his presence all about them it almost startled her visitor to hear no protest escape from her. She accepted his words ; he turned his eyes to her again to see in what manner she accepted them. It was with rising tears, and an extraordinary sweetness in the movement of putting out her hand to take his own. Nothing more wonderful had ever appeared to Stransom than, in that little chamber of remembrance and homage, to see her convey with such exquisite mildness that, as from Acton Hague, any injury was credible. The clock ticked in the stillness—Hague had probably given it to her—and while he let her hold his hand with a tenderness that was almost an assumption of responsibility for his old pain as well as his new, Stransom after a minute broke out : " Good God, how he must have used *you !* "

She dropped his hand at this, got up and, moving across the room, made straight a small picture to which, on examining it, he had given a slight push. Then, turning round on him, with her pale gayety recovered : " I've forgiven him ! " she declared.

" I know what you've done," said Stransom ; " I know what you've done for years." For a moment they looked at each other across the room, with their long community of service in their eyes. This short passage made, to Stransom's sense, for the woman before him, an immense, an absolutely naked confession ; which was presently, suddenly blushing red and changing her place again, what she appeared to become aware that he perceived in it. He got up. " How you must have loved him ! "

" Women are not like men. They can love even where they've suffered."

" Women are wonderful," said Stransom. " But I assure you I've forgiven him too."

" If I had known of any thing so strange I wouldn't have brought you here."

" So that we might have gone on in our ignorance to the last ? "

" What do you call the last ? " she asked, smiling still.

At this he could smile back at her. " You'll see—when it comes."

She reflected a moment. " This is better perhaps ; but as we were—it was good."

" Did it never happen that he spoke of me ? " Stransom enquired.

Considering more intently, she made no answer, and he quickly recognized that he would have been adequately answered by her asking how often he himself had spoken of their terrible friend. Suddenly a brighter light broke in her face, and an excited idea sprang to her lips in the question : " You *have* forgiven him ? "

" How, if I hadn't, could I linger here ? "

She winced, for an instant, at the deep but unintended irony of this ; but even while she did so she panted quickly :   " Then in the lights on your altar ? "

" There's never a light for Acton Hague ! "

She stared, with a great visible fall. " But if he's one of your Dead ? "

" He's one of the world's, if you like—he's one of yours. But he's not one of mine. Mine are only the Dead who died possessed of me.   They're mine in death because they were mine in life."

" *He* was yours in life, then, even if for a while he ceased to be. If you forgave him you went back to him.   Those whom we've once loved——"

" Are those who can hurt us most," Stransom broke in.

" Ah, it's not true—you've *not* forgiven him ! " she wailed, with a passion that startled him.

He looked at her a moment.   " What was it he did to you ? "

" Every thing ! "   Then abruptly she put out her hand in farewell.   " Good-by."

He turned as cold as he had turned that night he read of the death of Acton Hague.   " You mean that we meet no more ? "

" Not as we have met—not *there !* "

He stood aghast at this snap of their great bond, at the renouncement that rang out in the word she so passionately emphasized.   " But what's changed —for you ? "

She hesitated, in all the vividness of a trouble that, for the first time since he had known her, made her splendidly stern.   " How can you understand now when you didn't understand before ? "

" I didn't understand before only because I didn't know.   Now that I know, I see what I've been living with for years," Stransom went on very gently.

She looked at him with a larger allowance, as if

she appreciated his good-nature. " How can I, then, with this new knowledge of my own, ask you to continue to live with it ? "

" I set up my altar, with its multiplied meanings——" Stransom began ; but she quickly interrupted him :

" You set up your altar, and when I wanted one most I found it magnificently ready. I used it, with the gratitude I've always shown you, for I knew from of old that it was dedicated to Death. I told you, long ago, that my Dead were not many. Yours were, but all you had done for them was none too much for *my* worship ! You had placed a great light for Each—I gathered them together for One ! "

" We had simply different intentions," Stransom replied. " That, as you say, I perfectly knew, and I don't see why your intention shouldn't still sustain you."

" That's because you're generous—you can imagine and think. But the spell is broken."

It seemed to poor Stransom, in spite of his resistance, that it really was, and the prospect stretched gray and void before him. All, however, that he could say was : " I hope you'll try before you give up."

" If I had known you had ever known him, I should have taken for granted he had his candle," she presently rejoined. " What's changed, as you say, is that on making the discovery I find he never has had it. That makes *my* attitude "—she paused a moment, as if thinking how to express it, then said simply—"all wrong."

"Come once again," Stransom pleaded.

"Will you give him his candle?" she asked.

He hesitated, but only because it would sound ungracious; not because he had a doubt of his feeling. "I can't do that!" he declared at last.

"Then good-by." And she gave him her hand again.

He had got his dismissal; besides which, in the agitation of every thing that had opened out to him, he felt the need to recover himself as he could only do in solitude. Yet he lingered—lingered to see if she had no compromise to express, no attenuation to propose. But he only met her great lamenting eyes, in which indeed he read that she was as sorry for him as for any one else. This made him say : "At least, at any rate, I may see you here."

"Oh, yes! come if you like. But I don't think it will do."

Stransom looked round the room once more; he felt in truth by no means sure it would do. He felt also stricken and more and more cold, and his chill was like an ague in which he had to make an effort not to shake. "I must try on my side, if you can't try on yours," he dolefully rejoined. She came out with him to the hall and into the doorway, and here he put to her the question that seemed to him the one he could least answer from his own wit. "Why have you never let me come before?"

"Because my aunt would have seen you, and I should have had to tell her how I came to know you."

"And what would have been the objection to that?"

"It would have entailed other explanations; there would at any rate have been that danger."

"Surely she knew you went every day to church," Stransom objected.

"She didn't know what I went for."

"Of me then she never even heard?"

"You'll think I was deceitful. But I didn't need to be!"

Stransom was now on the lower doorstep, and his hostess held the door half-closed behind him. Through what remained of the opening he saw her framed face. He made a supreme appeal. "What *did* he do to you?"

"It would have come out—*she* would have told you. That fear, at my heart—that was my reason!" And she closed the door, shutting him out.

———

VIII

HE had ruthlessly abandoned her—that, of course, was what he had done. Stransom made it all out in solitude, at leisure, fitting the unmatched pieces gradually together and dealing one by one with a hundred obscure points. She had known Hague only after her present friend's relations with him had wholly terminated ; obviously indeed a good while after ; and it was natural enough that of his previous life she should have ascertained only what he had judged good to communicate. There were passages it was quite conceivable that even in moments of the tenderest expansion, he should have withheld. Of many facts in the career of a man so in the eye of the world there was of course a common knowledge ; but this lady lived apart from public affairs, and the only period perfectly clear to her would have been the period following the dawn of her own drama. A man, in her place, would have " looked up " the past— would even have consulted old newspapers. It remained singular indeed that in her long contact with the partner of her retrospect no accident had lighted a train ; but there was no arguing about that ; the accident had in fact come ; it had simply been that security had prevailed. She had taken what Hague had given her, and her blankness in respect of his other connections was only a touch in the picture of that plasticity Stransom had supreme reason to know so great a master could have been trusted to produce.

This picture, for a while, was all that our friend saw ; he caught his breath again and again as it came over him that the woman with whom he had had for years so fine a point of contact was a woman whom Acton Hague, of all men in the

15

world, had more or less fashioned. Such as she
sat there to-day, she was ineffaceably stamped with
him. Beneficent, blameless as Stransom held her,
he couldn't rid himself of the sense that he had been
the victim of a fraud. She had imposed upon him
hugely, though she had known it as little as he.
All this later past came back to him as a time grotesquely misspent. Such at least were his first
reflections; after a while he found himself more
divided and only, as the end of it, more troubled.
He imagined, recalled, reconstituted, figured out
for himself the truth she had refused to give him ;
the effect of which was to make her seem to him
only more saturated with her fate. He felt her
spirit, in the strange business, to be finer than his
own in the very degree in which she might have
been, in which she certainly had been, more wronged.
A woman, when she was wronged, was always more
wronged than a man, and there were conditions
when the least she could have got off with was
more than the most he could have to endure. He
was sure this rare creature wouldn't have got off
with the least. He was awe-struck at the thought
of such a surrender—such a prostration. Moulded
indeed she had been by powerful hands, to have
converted her injury into an exaltation so sublime.
The fellow had only had to die for every thing that
was ugly in him to be washed out in a torrent. It
was vain to try to guess what had taken place, but
nothing could be clearer than that she had ended
by accusing herself. She absolved him at every

point, she adored her very wounds. The passion
by which he had profited had rushed back after
its ebb, and now the tide of tenderness, arrested
forever at flood, was too deep even to fathom.
Stransom sincerely considered that he had forgiven
him ; but how little he had achieved the miracle that
she had achieved ! His forgiveness was silence,
but hers was mere unuttered sound. The light
she had demanded for his altar would have
broken his silence with a blare ; whereas all the
lights in the church were for her too great a hush.

She had been right about the difference—she
had spoken the truth about the change ; Stransom
felt before long that he was perversely but definitely jealous. *His* tide had ebbed, not flowed ;
if he had " forgiven " Acton Hague, that forgiveness was a motive with a broken spring. The very
fact of her appeal for a material sign, a sign that
should make her dead lover equal there with the
others, presented the concession to Stransom as
too handsome for the case. He had never thought
of himself as hard, but an exorbitant article might
easily render him so. He moved round and round
this one, but only in widening circles—the more
he looked at it the less acceptable it appeared. At
the same time he had no illusion about the effect
of his refusal ; he perfectly saw that it was the
beginning of a separation. He left her alone for
many days ; but when at last he called upon her
again this conviction acquired a depressing force.
In the interval he had kept away from the church,

and he needed no fresh assurance from her to know
she had not entered it. The change was complete
enough ; it had broken up her life. Indeed it had
broken up his, for all the fires of his shrine seemed
to him suddenly to have been quenched. A great
indifference fell upon him, the weight of which
was in itself a pain ; and he never knew what his
devotion had been for him till, in that shock, it
stopped like a dropped watch. Neither did he
know with how large a confidence he had counted
on the final service that had now failed ; the mortal
deception was that in this abandonment the whole
future gave way.

These days of her absence proved to him of what
she was capable ; all the more that he never
dreamed she was vindictive or even resentful. It
was not in anger she had forsaken him ; it was in
absolute submission to hard reality, to crude des-
tiny. This came home to him when he sat with
her again in the room in which her late aunt's conversation lingered like the tone of a cracked
piano. She tried to make him forget how much
they were estranged ; but in the very presence of
what they had given up it was impossible not to
be sorry for her. He had taken from her so much
more than she had taken from him. He argued
with her again, told her she could now have the
altar to herself ; but she only shook her head with
pleading sadness, begging him not to waste his
breath on the impossible, the extinct. Couldn't he
see that, in relation to her private need, the rites

he had established were practically an elaborate
exclusion ? She regretted nothing that had happened ; it had all been right so long as she didn't
know, and it was only that now she knew too
much, and that from the moment their eyes were
open they would simply have to conform. It had
doubtless been happiness enough for them to go
on together so long. She was gentle, grateful,
resigned ; but this was only the form of a deep
immutability. He saw that he should never more
cross the threshold of the second room, and he felt
how much this alone would make a stranger of him
and give a conscious stiffness to his visits. He
would have hated to plunge again into that well of
reminders, but he enjoyed quite as little the vacant
alternative.

After he had been with her three or four times
it seemed to him that to have come at last into her
house had had the horrid effect of diminishing
their intimacy. He had known her better, had
liked her in greater freedom, when they merely
walked together or kneeled together. Now they
only pretended ; before they had been nobly sin-
cere. They began to try their walks again, but it
proved a lame imitation, for these things, from the
first, beginning or ending, had been connected
with their visits to the church. They had either
strolled away as they came out or had gone in to
rest on the return. Besides, Stransom now grew
weary ; he couldn't walk as of old. The omission
made every thing false ; it was a horrible mutila-

tion of their lives. Our friend was frank and
monotonous ; he made no mystery of his remon-
strance and no secret of his predicament. Her
response, whatever it was, always came to the
same thing—an implied invitation to him to judge,
if he spoke of predicaments, of how much comfort
she had in hers. For him indeed there was no
comfort even in complaint, for every allusion to
what had befallen them only made the author of
their trouble more present. Acton Hague was
between them, that was the essence of the matter ;
and he was never so much between them as when
they were face to face. Stransom, even while he
wanted to banish him, had the strangest sense of
desiring a satisfaction that could come only from
having accepted him. Deeply disconcerted by
what he knew, he was still worse tormented by
really not knowing. Perfectly aware that it would
have been horribly vulgar to abuse his old friend
or to tell his companion the story of their quarrel,
it yet vexed him that her depth of reserve should
give him no opening and should have the effect of
a magnanimity greater even than his own.

He challenged himself, denounced himself, asked
himself if he were in love with her that he should
care so much what adventures she had had. He
had never for a moment admitted that he was in
love with her ; therefore nothing could have surprised him more than to discover that he was
jealous. What but jealousy could give a man that
sore, contentious wish to have the detail of what

would make him suffer ? Well enough he knew
indeed that he should never have it from the only
person who, to-day, could give it to him. She let
him press her with his sombre eyes, only smiling
at him with an exquisite mercy and breathing
equally little the word that would expose her
secret and the word that would appear to deny his
literal right to bitterness. She told nothing, she
judged nothing; she accepted every thing but
the possibility of her return to the old symbols.
Stransom divined that for her, too, they had been
vividly individual, had stood for particular hours
or particular attributes—particular links in her
chain. He made it clear to himself, as he believed,
that his difficulty lay in the fact that the very
nature of the plea for his faithless friend constituted a prohibition; that it happened to have
come from *her* was precisely the vice that attached
to it. To the voice of impersonal generosity he
felt sure he would have listened ; he would have
deferred to an advocate who, speaking from
abstract justice, knowing of his omission, without
having known Hague, should have had the imagination to say : " Oh, remember only the best of
him ; pity him ; provide for him ! " To provide
for him on the very ground of having discovered
another of his turpitudes was not to pity him, but
to glorify him. The more Stransom thought, the
more he made it out that this relation of Hague's,
whatever it was, could only have been a deception
finely practised. Where had it come into the life

that all men saw ? Why had he never heard of it,
if it had had the frankness of an attitude honorable ? Stransom knew enough of his other ties, of
his obligations and appearances, not to say enough
of his general character, to be sure there had been
some infamy. In one way or another the poor
woman had been coldly sacrificed. That was why,
at the last as well as the first, he must still leave
him out.

IX

AND yet this was no solution, especially after
he had talked again to his friend of all it had
been his plan that she should finally do for him.
He had talked in the other days, and she had
responded with a frankness qualified only by a
courteous reluctance—a reluctance that touched
him—to linger on the question of his death. She
had then practically accepted the charge, suffered
him to feel that he could depend upon her to be
the eventual guardian of his shrine ; and it was in
the name of what had so passed between them that
he appealed to her not to forsake him in his old
age. She listened to him now with a sort of shining coldness and all her habitual forbearance to
insist on her terms ; her deprecation was even still
tenderer, for it expressed the compassion of her
own sense that he was abandoned. Her terms,
however, remained the same, and scarcely the less

audible for not being uttered ; although he was sure that, secretly, even more than he, she felt bereft of the satisfaction his solemn trust was to have provided for her. They both missed the rich future, but she missed it most, because, after all, it was to have been entirely hers ; and it was her acceptance of the loss that gave him the full measure of her preference for the thought of Acton Hague over any other thought whatever. He had humor enough to laugh rather grimly when he said to himself : " Why the deuce does she like him so much more than she likes me ?"— the reasons being really so conceivable. But even his faculty of analysis left the irritation standing, and this irritation proved perhaps the greatest misfortune that had ever overtaken him. There had been nothing yet that made him so much want to give up. He had of course by this time well reached the age of renouncement ; but it had not hitherto been vivid to him that it was time to give up every thing.

Practically, at the end of six months, he had renounced the friendship that was once so charming and comforting. His privation had two faces, and the face it had turned to him on the occasion of his last attempts to cultivate that friendship was the one he could look at least. This was the privation he inflicted ; the other was the privation he bore. The conditions she never phrased he used to murmur to himself in solitude : " One more, one more—only just one." Certainly he was

going down ; he often felt it when he caught himself, over his work, staring at vacancy and giving
voice to that inanity. There was proof enough
besides in his being so weak and so ill. His irritation took the form of melancholy, and his melancholy that of the conviction that his health had
quite failed. His altar, moreover, had ceased to
exist ; his chapel, in his dreams, was a great dark
cavern. All the lights had gone out—all his Dead
had died again. He couldn't exactly see at first
how it had been in the power of his late companion
to extinguish them, since it was neither for her nor
by her that they had been called into being. Then
he understood that it was essentially in his own
soul the revival had taken place, and that in the
air of this soul they were now unable to breathe.
The candles might mechanically burn, but each of
them had lost its lustre. The church had become
a void ; it was his presence, her presence, their
common presence, that had made the indispensable
medium. If any thing was wrong every thing
was—her silence spoiled the tune.

Then, when three months were gone, he felt so
lonely that he went back ; reflecting that as they
had been his best society for years his Dead perhaps wouldn't let him forsake them without doing
something more for him. They stood there, as he
had left them, in their tall radiance, the bright
cluster that had already made him, on occasions
when he was willing to compare small things with
great, liken them to a group of sea-lights on the

edge of the ocean of life. It was a relief to him,
after a while, as he sat there, to feel that they had
still a virtue. He was more and more easily tired,
and he always drove now ; the action of his heart
was weak, and gave him none of the reassurance
conferred by the action of his fancy. None the
less he returned yet again, returned several times,
and finally, during six months, haunted the place
with a renewal of frequency and a strain of impatience. In winter the church was unwarmed,
and exposure to cold was forbidden him, but the
glow of his shrine was an influence in which he
could almost bask. He sat and wondered to what
he had reduced his absent associate, and what she
now did with the hours of her absence. There were
other churches, there were other altars, there were
other candles ; in one way or another her piety
would still operate ; he couldn't absolutely have
deprived her of her rites. So he argued, but without contentment ; for he well enough knew there
was no other such rare semblance of the mountain
of light she had once mentioned to him as the
satisfaction of her need. As this semblance again
gradually grew great to him and his pious practice
more regular, there was a sharper and sharper pang
for him in the imagination of her darkness ; for
never so much as in these weeks had his rites been
real, never had his gathered company seemed so to
respond and even to invite. He lost himself in the
large lustre, which was more and more what he
had from the first wished it to be—as dazzling as

the vision of heaven in the mind of a child. He
wandered in the fields of light ; he passed, among
the tall tapers, from tier to tier, from fire to fire,
from name to name, from the white intensity of
one clear emblem, of one saved soul, to another.
It was in the quiet sense of having saved his souls
that his deep, strange instinct rejoiced. This was
no dim theological rescue, no boon of a contingent
world ; they were saved better than faith or works
could save them, saved for the warm world they
had shrunk from dying to, for actuality, for continuity, for the certainty of human remembrance.

By this time he had survived all his friends ;
the last straight flame was three years old ; there
was no one to add to the list. Over and over he
called his roll, and it appeared to him compact
and complete. Where should he put in another ;
where, if there were no other objection, would it
stand in its place in the rank ? He reflected, with
a want of sincerity of which he was quite conscious, that it would be difficult to determine that
place. More and more, besides, face to face with
his little legion, reading over endless histories,
handling the empty shells and playing with the
silence—more and more he could see that he had
never introduced an alien. He had had his great
compassions, his indulgences—there were cases in
which they had been immense ; but what had his
devotion after all been, if it hadn't been fundamentally a respect ? He was, however, himself
surprised at his stiffness ; by the end of the winter

the responsibility of it was what was uppermost in
his thoughts. The refrain had grown old to them,
the plea for just one more. There came a day
when, for simple exhaustion, if symmetry should
really demand just one more, he was ready to take
symmetry into account. Symmetry was harmony,
and the idea of harmony began to haunt him ; he
said to himself that harmony was of course every
thing. He took, in fancy, his composition to
pieces, redistributing it into other lines, making
other juxtapositions and contrasts. He shifted
this and that candle ; he made the spaces different ;
he effaced the disfigurement of a possible gap.
There were subtle and complex relations, a scheme
of cross-reference, and moments in which he
seemed to catch a glimpse of the void so sensible
to the woman who wandered in exile or sat where
he had seen her with the portrait of Acton Hague.
Finally, in this way, he arrived at a conception of
the total, the ideal, which left a clear opportunity
for just another figure. " Just one more, to round
it off ; just one more, just one," continued to hum
itself in his head. There was a strange confusion
in the thought, for he felt the day to be near when
he too should be one of the Others. What, in this
case, would the Others matter to him, since they
only mattered to the living ? Even as one of the
Dead, what would his altar matter to him, since
his particular dream of keeping it up had melted
away ? What had harmony to do with the case, if
his lights were all to be quenched ? What he had

hoped for was an instituted thing. He might per-
petuate it on some other pretext, but his special
meaning would have dropped. This meaning was
to have lasted with the life of the one other person
who understood it.

In March he had an illness during which he
spent a fortnight in bed, and when he revived a
little he was told of two things that had happened.
One was that a lady, whose name was not known
to the servants (she left none), had been three times
to ask about him ; the other was that in his sleep,
and on an occasion when his mind evidently wandered, he was heard to murmur again and again :
" Just one more—just one." As soon as he found
himself able to go out, and before the doctor in
attendance had pronounced him so, he drove to see
the lady who had come to ask about him. She
was not at home ; but this gave him the opportunity, before his strength should fail again, to
take his way to the church. He entered the church
alone ; he had declined, in a happy manner he possessed of being able to decline effectively, the company of his servant or of a nurse. He knew now
perfectly what these good people thought ; they
had discovered his clandestine connection, the
magnet that had drawn him for so many years,
and doubtless attached a significance of their own
to the odd words they had repeated to him. The
nameless lady was the clandestine connection—a
fact nothing could have made clearer than his in-
decent haste to rejoin her. He sank on his knees

before his altar, and his head fell over on his hands.
His weakness, his life's weariness, overtook him.
It seemed to him he had come for the great surrender. At first he asked himself how he should
get away; then, with the failing belief in the
power, the very desire to move gradually left him.
He had come, as he always came, to lose himself;
the fields of light were still there to stray in; only
this time, in straying, he would never come back.
He had given himself to his Dead, and it was
good; this time his Dead would keep him. He
couldn't rise from his knees; he believed he
should never rise again; all he could do was to
lift his face and fix his eyes upon his lights. They
looked unusually, strangely splendid, but the one
that always drew him most had an unprecedented.
lustre. It was the central voice of the choir, the
glowing heart of the brightness, and on this occasion it seemed to expand, to spread great wings of
flame. The whole altar flared—it dazzled and
blinded; but the source of the vast radiance
burned clearer than the rest; it gathered itself
into form, and the form was human beauty and
human charity; it was the far-off face of Mary
Antrim. She smiled at him from the glory of
heaven—she brought the glory down with her to
take him. He bowed his head in submission, and
at the same moment another wave rolled over him.
Was it the quickening of joy to pain? In the
midst of his joy, at any rate, he felt his buried
face grow hot as with some communicated knowl-

edge that had the force of a reproach. It suddenly
made him contrast that very rapture with the bliss
he had refused to another. This breath of the
passion immortal was all that other had asked;
the descent of Mary Antrim opened his spirit with
a great compunctious throb for the descent of
Acton Hague. It was as if Stransom had read
what her eyes said to him.

After a moment he looked round him in a despair which made him feel as if the source of life
were ebbing. The church had been empty—he
was alone; but he wanted to have something
done, to make a last appeal. This idea gave him
strength for an effort; he rose to his feet with a
movement that made him turn, supporting himself
by the back of a bench. Behind him was a prostrate figure, a figure he had seen before; a woman
in deep mourning, bowed in grief or in prayer.
He had seen her in other days—the first time he
came into the church, and he slightly wavered
there, looking at her again till she seemed to become aware he had noticed her. She raised her
head and met his eyes : the partner of his long
worship was there. She looked across at him an
instant with a face wondering and scared ; he saw
that he had given her an alarm. Then quickly
rising, she came straight to him with both hands out.

"Then you *could* come? God sent you !" he
murmured, with a happy smile.

"You're very ill—you shouldn't be here," she
urged, in anxious reply.

"God sent me too, I think. I was ill when I came, but the sight of you does wonders." He held her hands, and they steadied and quickened him. "I've something to tell you."

"Don't tell me!" she tenderly pleaded; "let me tell you. This afternoon, by a miracle, the sweetest of miracles, the sense of our difference left me. I was out—I was near, thinking, wandering alone, when, on the spot, something changed in my heart. It's my confession—there it is. To come back, to come back on the instant—the idea gave me wings. It was as if I suddenly saw something —as if it all became possible. I could come for what you yourself came for: that was enough. So here I am. It's not for my own—that's over. But I'm here for *them*." And breathless, infinitely relieved by her low, precipitate explanation, she looked with eyes that reflected all its splendor at the magnificence of their altar.

"They're here for you," Stransom said, "they're present to-night as they've never been. They speak for you—don't you see?—in a passion of light—they sing out like a choir of angels. Don't you hear what they say?—they offer the very thing you asked of me."

"Don't talk of it—don't think of it; forget it!" She spoke in hushed supplication, and while the apprehension deepened in her eyes she disengaged one of her hands and passed an arm round him, to support him better, to help him to sink into a seat.

16

He let himself go, resting on her ; he dropped upon the bench, and she fell on her knees beside him with his arm on her shoulder. So he remained an instant, staring up at his shrine. "They say there's a gap in the array—they say it's not full, complete. Just one more," he went on, softly— "isn't that what you wanted ? Yes, one more, one more."

"Ah, no more—no more !" she wailed, as if with a quick, new horror of it, under her breath.

"Yes, one more," he repeated simply ; "just one !" And with this his head dropped on her shoulder ; she felt that in his weakness he had fainted. But alone with him in the dusky church a great dread was on her of what might still happen, for his face had the whiteness of death.

THE END